TH DAVIDSON FILE

Compiled from the personal papers of His Grace
the Lord Caiaphas, High Priest of Jewry

by

Stuart Jackman

Published by

LUTTERWORTH PRESS   Guildford   Surrey

First Published 1982

ISBN 0-7188-2526-8

Printed and bound in Great Britain by
MACKAYS OF CHATHAM LTD

KEY TO FILE CONTENTS

THE ROYAL PALACE
THE OFFICE OF THE HIGH PRIEST

MEMORANDUM

TO MY SUCCESSOR IN THE OFFICE OF HIGH PRIEST

The contents of this file have been collected over the years to provide an outline of the career of Jesus Davidson of Nazareth from his birth in Bethlehem to his execution on a charge of treason in Jerusalem.

The letters and transcripts represent only a small selection from the material made available to me from the files of the Special Intelligence Section of the Imperial Roman Army and those of our own Police HQ's Y Dept. Some are originals, some photostats. They are, however, sufficient to trace the progress of Davidson's abortive attempt to have himself proclaimed Messiah. They give some indication of the kind of disruptive element he introduced into the lives of ordinary people as well as of the very real threat he posed to the safety of the realm.

Whilst not all the questions raised in this file have been answered to my entire satisfaction I remain convinced that the action I was compelled to take in order to rid the nation of this man was the right one (however uncertain the Governor-General may have been - vide Item 18).

It is my firm belief that the assurance I gave to Lord Pilate in my letter following the demonstration mounted by Davidson's followers at the Feast of Weeks (Item 27) have subsequently been fully justified.

Caiaphas

Caiaphas

High Priest.

THE IMPERIAL ROMAN ARMY

EXECUTIONS

NAME: Davidson, Jesus	DATE OF BIRTH: 25.12.48

PLACE OF BIRTH:
Bethlehem, Judea

OCCUPATION:
Carpenter (unemployed)

FATHER'S NAME: Not known	MOTHER'S NAME: Mary ? Married Joseph Davidson 12.9.48

ADDRESS AT TIME OF ARREST:
NFA (No fixed abode)

DATE OF ARREST: 21.4.81	PLACE OF ARREST: Gethsemane, Jerusalem E2

CHARGE(S):

Treason

DATE OF TRIAL:

21/22.4.81

VERDICT:
Guilty as charged

SENTENCE:
Execution

SENTENCE CONFIRMED BY:
H.E. the Lord Pilate, Governor-General

DATE AND PLACE OF EXECUTION:
22.4.81   Skull Hill, Jerusalem

OFFICER i/c EXECUTION SQUAD:
Lieutenant Q.A. Geller, A Company, 10th Legion

SIGNED: *G.A. Geller. Lt.*

UNIVERSITY OF BABYLON
FACULTY OF SCIENCE & TECHNOLOGY

Telephone 358933
OFFICE:

Deputy Chancellor

PHOTOCOPIED
15 NOV 48
DATE
SIGNED *A L Habbuk*

DEPARTMENT OF
ASTRO-PHYSICS
CHALDEAN COURT
BABYLON

Dr. C. Y. Melchoir PhD. BSc. MEng. FRASP

12th November '48

POSTAL SURVEILLANCE DEPT
ISS STATE SECURITY P

The Chancellor,
Senate House,
University Square,
Nineveh.

Dear Clem,

About this Cyrus Memorial Lecture on January 5. Look, Clem, you don't want me for this. I mean, I appreciate the honour and it's damned nice of you to ask me, but it's a job for a scholar not a technician. And that's all I am really. Don't let the PhD fool you. I'm just a technician - the junior member of a team working on a bit of research in the field of astro-physics. My colleagues Dr Caspar and Professor Balthazar now - either of them would fill the bill for you. But not me. Caspar's probably the top man in the Space-Light-Time sector. And Balthazar is into UFO sighting investigation and analysis in the biggest possible way. Me, I'm just a nuts-and-bolts man.

In any case, even if I felt I could come up to your expectations, the date of the lecture rules me out. Rules the three of us out, come to that.

It's all very hush-hush at the moment (for your eyes only, as they say) but the fact is we've discovered a new star - actually a new kind of star. At least Caspar thinks it's a star; Balthazar thinks it's a kind of super-UFO; and I'm keeping an open mind. Whatever it is, it's important and we can't afford to lose track of it. It's travelling in an

east/west orbit and the three of us leave tomorrow on what
may well prove to be a long and difficult trip.   At this stage
it's impossible to predict our final destination but if my
calculations are anything like accurate we expect to find
ourselves in or near Jerusalem about the time you'll be gather-
ing for the Memorial Lecture.

I don't want to say too much about what we expect to
find.   As of now it's all highly speculative.   But this I
will tell you (in strict confidence): we think the star will
lead us to what the sci-fi scribblers call a close encounter
of the third kind.   Just writing that down fills me with
doubts.   I have all the physicist's built-in caution about
these things.   But in Balthazar's view it's some sort of space
vehicle which is bringing a VIP from another world.   Caspar
is inclined to niggle over the terminology.   He thinks it's a
star which has somehow strayed into our galaxy and must be
regarded as a natural phenomenon with supernatural implications.
But they are both firmly convinced that a king is about to
arrive from somewhere out there on the edge of the universe.
Balthazar thinks he knows how, Caspar is not so sure.   But
both agree a king is coming.   Not just to rule over Israel
(although, from what we hear of Herod, it's high time that
country had somebody with a bit of integrity to run its affairs)
but to rule over the world.   A King of kings, in fact.

I know - it's crazy.   But it is a strange star.   Damned
strange.   For one thing, its velocity is sub-sonic.   It's a
slow star, Clem.   And that's impossible.   It arrived in orbit
at the speed of light and immediately became virtually motionless.
It defies all our attempts to classify it.   When we feed its
data into our computers all hell breaks loose.   Its response

to radio signals is eccentric.   Only its track remains
constant and predictable.   We are setting out tomorrow
with nothing more than that to go on.

All of which, intriguing as it is, pales into insig-
nificance when set against our speculations concerning the
reasons for its arrival.   The advent of a super-king carries
over-tones of immense importance - political rather than
scientific.   His arrival could mean peace and fulfilment for
humanity.   An end to our troubles in a greedy, angry world.
Or it could precipitate a crisis of global proportions which
will affect the lives of people in every nation for centuries
to come.   Peace or global war?   Fascinating - and frightening - alternatives.

Three boffins travelling through the winter weather in
pursuit of a star.   It sounds ridiculous, doesn't it?   A
zany episode from some latter-day Arabian Nights.   But we
are going.   Putting our trust in our instruments and calculations - and going.   We shall take suitable gifts, of course.
Gold and frankincense and myrrh - tokens of this planet's
wealth, religious insight and mortality.   If Balthazar is
right and the star is indeed a UFO carrying a VIP from outer
space, it will perhaps be appropriate to offer him such gifts.
Even if, as Caspar believes, we'll find a new-born child at
our journey's end.   The gold and myrrh I go along with.   But
I'm less happy about the frankincense.   Probably because I
cannot reconcile science and religion.   But the old super-
stitions die hard in even the most logical of minds and God -
if there is a God - knows we need another dimension in our
personalities if we are to preserve our basic humanity.   You
can, after all, admire a computor.   But you can't worship it.
And I find, rather to my surprise, that a part of me still

4.

hungers for something - or someone - to worship.　Maybe this
damned star's beginning to get to me.

Since Jerusalem appears to be the most likely location
of the visitation we plan to consult with Herod on our arrival
there and hope to find him co-operative.　Probably a vain hope.
How will a puppet-king with his temperament react to the arrival
of a super-monarch in his territory?　But Caspar says these are
political speculations and not really our concern.　I hope he's
right.

Well, there it is, Clem.　I'll keep you posted about the
outcome of our journey.　Thanks again for inviting me to
address your savants.　It's not really my scene, even if I
were free to come.　But next year Balthazar or Caspar might
well have something juicy to talk about - if you can pin them
down.　If things go as we expect, they'll be booked solid for
the rest of their lives.

Yours,

THE IMPERIAL ROMAN ARMY

ARMY HEADQUARTERS · ANTONIA TOWER JERUSALEM

D Section ~~SECRET~~ Special Intelligence

CLASSIFIED MATERIAL   MOST SECRET

EXCERPT FROM A TRANSCRIPTION OF TAPED INTERROGATION SESSION
26.12.48

CLASSIFIED

NAME OF SUSPECT:	CAMON, PETER
AGE:	53
OCCUPATION:	HEAD SHEPHERD
DATE & PLACE ARRESTED:	HOME FARM, DAVID'S LANE, BETHLEHEM
INTERROGATOR:	LIEUTENANT B.L. MARIUS

(EXCERPT COMMENCES 23.00 HOURS APPROX)

MARIUS: All right, let's go back to this light in the
            sky. When exactly did it first appear?

CAMON: I dunno exactly. About two in the morning.

MARIUS: You look tired, Mr Camon. Are you?

CAMON: Yes.

MARIUS: Over in the east, was it?

CAMON: What?

MARIUS: The light in the sky.

CAMON: Oh. Yes, in the east. Look, I've told you all
            this.

MARIUS: So tell me again. From the beginning. It's
            the night of the 24th, right? And you were -
            where was it you were?

CAMON: Up in the north pasture. We was all there, all
            six of us, sitting round the fire with the ewes
            penned in the hollow below us and ....

MARIUS: This light - it was moving was it?

CAMON: Yes. It was big and low down in the sky, coming in towards us over the town. And there was this noise, see? Sort of booming and whistling.

MARIUS: A jet on full take-off power.

CAMON: That's what I thought at first. Hullo, I sez, this boy's cutting it a bit fine over these hills. I mean, it was right down, see, close to the ground, not more than maybe a hundred feet above us. But it warn't no jet, sir, leastways not unless it blew up.

MARIUS: Blew up? You mean it exploded?

CAMON: Right over our heads. Spread all over the sky the light were, bright as day and the noise fit to split your skull open. And going on and on, see? Not like one big bang and finish. This just kept on howling and shrieking, getting louder every second.

MARIUS: And that's when you heard the voice, is it?

CAMON: When they heard it, yes, sir. The others, not me. I didn't hear no voice, not with all that racket battering away at me. Look, I told you twice now, if there was a voice I didn't hear it. It's the others you want to ask, not me.

MARIUS: Oh, we will, Mr Camon. We will. Now about this child.

CAMON: Ah, he were there all right. In the stable behind the pub down the bottom of the High Street.

MARIUS: You saw him, did you?

CAMON: You're trying to trap me, aren't you? No, I didn't see him. The others shoved off but I stayed on the hill. We'd got close on three hundred ewes up there, all of them carrying, see? Somebody had to stay with them. And I'm head shepherd after all.

MARIUS: What made them think the baby was a king?

CAMON: Well, that were the angel, warn't it? This voice they reckon spoke to them out of the sky, like.

MARIUS: But you didn't hear it?

CAMON: For pity's sake, how many more times? No, I didn't hear it.

MARIUS: So what you're really saying is - these men with you thought they heard a voice telling them to go and see a new king born in a stable. Is that right?

CAMON: That's correct, sir, yes. And when they came back they said they'd seen him, just like the voice said.

MARIUS: Was the light still there then?

CAMON: No, sir. It went away right after the voice spoke.

MARIUS: The voice you didn't hear?

CAMON: Yes.

MARIUS: How did the light go away?

CAMON: Well, it - I dunno - it just vanished, like. I mean, I didn't see it go. I had my hands over my eyes, didn't I? A light as bright as that could blind a man. And then, when the noise stopped and I took my hands away, it was all dark again. No light, no noise, nothing.

MARIUS: A voice you didn't hear. A baby you never saw. A light that just vanished. I'm disappointed in you, Mr Camon. This is the third time we've been through your story and always you tell me the same stupid lies.

CAMON: No, sir. It's the truth. That's exactly how it was.

MARIUS: So what is your explanation?

CAMON: I dunno, sir.

MARIUS: It doesn't make sense to you?

CAMON: Not really, sir, no.

MARIUS: Nor to me, Mr Camon, nor to me. On the other
            hand, there is a perfectly reasonable explanation.

CAMON: Yes, sir?

MARIUS: Oh yes. It goes like this. You all got cold and
            tired up there on the hill, so the others went
            down into the town and round to the back door of
            the pub and inside for a drink and a warm.

CAMON: They wouldn't do that, sir. Not my lads. Any-
            way, I wouldn't let them.

MARIUS: I'm sure you wouldn't. But you didn't know, did
            you? So they had to make up some ridiculous
            story about lights and voices and babies.

CAMON: But there was a baby in the stable.

MARIUS: I know. We've checked.

CAMON: There you are, then. I told you.

MARIUS: A peasant couple from up north, down here for the
            census and the woman pregnant and nowhere for
            them to go except the stable behind the pub.

CAMON: So my lads were telling the truth.

MARIUS: Were they? Oh, they saw the baby all right. And
            it was just what they needed. A tailor-made
            alibi for running out on you and the sheep. Add
            a few frills - angel voices and mysterious new
            kings - and they were in the clear. And you know
            that as well as I do.

CAMON: You think I'm covering for them, don't you?

MARIUS: I KNOW you're covering for them.

CAMON: But - wait a bit - what about the light? And the
            noise? I mean, I saw ....

MARIUS: What you saw and heard was Imperial Airways flight 69 out of Lydda for Alexandria. Take-off 02.00 hours. We've checked.

CAMON: No sir. Whatever it were it warn't no jet. And what about the voice? What about that, eh?

MARIUS: Voice? What voice? I thought you said you didn't hear a voice?

CAMON: No. Well I - no, I didn't hear ...

MARIUS: Precisely.

CAMON: If that's what you think, why have I been arrested?

MARIUS: You're not under arrest, Mr Camon. You're simply helping us with our enquiries.

CAMON: But .... You mean I'm free to go?

MARIUS: You would be, Mr Camon, you would be. If only ...

CAMON: If only what? For pity's sake, sir, I can't take much more of this. I haven't slept for two nights now and ...

MARIUS: If only you hadn't gone along with this absurd story about a new king. You see, a bunch of shepherds sneaking off for a drink - well, that's not our problem. But once you start spreading rumours about angels and voices and kings being born - well, we're interested. Because that's treason, Mr Camon. There's only one king in Judea and he's right here in the palace in Jerusalem, not skulking about in some stable in Bethlehem. Am I right?

CAMON: Yes, sir, I suppose so.

MARIUS: You suppose so?

CAMON: No, I mean, you're right, of course.

MARIUS: Good. So now, if you'll just sign this statement saying the whole story's a pack of lies, we can both go home and get some sleep.

CAMON: No. I don't know much about kings and that, but I

know my lads. And if they say there was a
voice telling them about the baby, well, sir,
I dunno how - but there was a voice.

MARIUS: I see.

CAMON: And another thing, sir, with respect. That
light in the sky warn't what you said. I know
what a jet looks like in the night sky and this
was something different.

MARIUS: Mr Camon, I'm a very patient man, but I do
sincerely hope you are not going to try my
patience by suggesting that what you saw was a
UFO?

CAMON: A what, sir?

MARIUS: Unidentified Flying Object. Little green men
with horns and six arms all the way from Venus.

CAMON: I dunno about that, sir. You see some pretty
strange things in the sky up there on the hill
at night.

MARIUS: Yes, I'm sure. You're not prepared to sign the
statement then?

CAMON: No, sir. I'm sorry, but - no.

MARIUS: In that case I'm afraid we'll just have to start
again at the beginning won't we? Now, you were
up in the north pasture and ....

EXCERPT ENDS

INTERROGATOR'S NOTE: Subsequent use of more forcible methods
failed to persuade Camon to change his story.
Whilst rejecting the evidence of the other
shepherds concerning the voice and the identity
of the child born in the stable, I am inclined to
believe Camon saw something unusual in the sky
that night. Query comet or meteor. Suggest tests
for radio-active poisoning of sheep and ground in
north pasture.

CLASSIFIED SECRET

6th January '49

12 Hill Lane
Bethlehem
Judea

Tel. 27356

Dear Matt

Boy, has this been a year to remember? First off, back in
April, Ruth finds she's expecting. After five years of marriage,
yet. So we convert the spare room into a nursery, put a down-
payment on the pram and she gets stuck into the knitting bit.
So what happens? Come September I get promoted and transferred
down here to Bethlehem. So we find a house (and a buyer for ours),
move in, check on the local quack and midwife and relax. Then
along comes this damned census malarky and we have to trek back
all the way to Tiberius just to stick our names on some bureaucratic
Roman form. Ruth as big as a battleship and the weather diabolical.
Not funny, mate.

OK. So we cope. It's a hassle, but we cope. Get back down
here just in time. Right on schedule, along comes Junior. Eight
pounds two ounces, black hair and brass lungs. No problems. No
complications. We have ourselves a son. John Matthew. Which is
were you come in, old lad.

The thing is, we're having a bit of a do this next weekend.
Nothing flash. Just the family and a few close friends. Just to
wet the baby's head. So what about it? Can you make it? Friday
afternoon and stay over till Sunday. I know it's a helluva long
way but it's in a good cause. And we ARE calling him after you.

By the way, d'you remember old Prof Balthazar? Tall, thin
character with a black beard, Used to lecture in astro-physics
when we were in college. Bulging with brains. No small talk. Got
him? Well he was here a couple of days ago. I was down in the town
one night about ten - buying a bottle of gripe-water from the all-
night chemist, actually. John Matthew's hooked on the stuff - and
the old Prof comes stalking up the street in a fur hat and the
sort of overcoat no horse would be seen dead in. He had a couple of
chaps with him and they were in a hell of a hurry. But I stopped
him and said hullo. He didn't recognise me, of course - I mean,
it's a year or two now since we were undergrads, isn't it? But
when I said I'd been in his tutorial group he thawed a bit. Said
maybe I could help them.

They were looking for a new king, he said. Just born. I thought he
meant our laddie for a moment - sort of academic joke, you know. I
mean, the old boy never did have much of a sense of humour, but he
did try. Anyway, it wasn't that. A joke, I mean. He was dead serious.
Seems they had come all the way from Persia to find this king.

Of course I said I knew nothing about it. Kings don't get themselves born in an over-grown village like Bethlehem. We don't run to palaces here, I said. I also said Herod wouldn't exactly be jumping for joy about it, if it was true. But Balthazar said, on the contrary, they'd been to see the old monster and he was dead keen to come over and pay his respects, once they had located the child.

Anyway, he thanked me and the three of them shoved off. And that was that. Obviously they never found anything. It would have been all over the town if they had. Funny, though, wasn't it?

Well, see you Friday. Boy, we'll really push the boat out, Matt. Imagine me a father. John Matthew's a great kid, although I say it myself. Full of life and energy and always smiling. I can't wait for him to grow up. I've got plans for this boy, Matt. Big plans.

By the way, don't say anything to Ruth, will you? About Balthazar, I mean. The thing is, she worries about the boy. Scared stiff something's going to happen to him. In Bethlehem, yet. It's only natural, I suppose. Post-natal depression. And she's always been a bit psychic. She came in from the clinic just this afternoon looking a touch frail. Said she'd heard the Tenth Legion's going to move in on the town tomorrow. I told her it'll be just a training exercise or something. I mean, what else? She calmed down a bit then. Looked sheepish. I said, 'What did you think they were coming for?' And she just shook her head.

Women. They worry when they don't have kids. And worry when they do. Anyway, that's how she is just now, Matt. Puts two and two together and makes five. So mum's the word about the old Prof's mythical king. OK?

Till Friday, then.

Joseph.

22.1.49

To: Dr. T.L.Hendrix,
      Imperial Physics Laboratory,
      Alexandria,
      Egypt.

From: Gregory Patros,
        Geophysical Research Officer,
        Project 23,
        Bethlehem,
        Judea.

Dear Theo,

I enclose my report on the Bethlehem project.

My findings, as you will see, are inconclusive. There is no scientific evidence to support the claims of the Judean Government concerning the deaths of the children. Unfortunately, because of the panic measures taken at the time - in particular the cremation order - it has not been possible to perform any postmortem examinations. Attempts to elicit accurate information from the parents of the dead children - symptoms, nature of the sickness, time factor - proved abortive. They are not, of course, trained in the scientific observation of the progress of radiation poisoning. I did not expect that they would be. But I did expect some co-operation. None was forthcoming. The whole town is in a state of shock - understandable in the circumstances - but my feeling is that there is something else which prevents them from discussing the incident. Fear, perhaps? But of what?

Can it be that we are dealing here with something political rather than scientific? Is the whole story of a mysterious star and the subsequent epidemic of radiation sickness really a cover-up for something else? I don't know. I append brief notes of two interviews I was able to conduct. I'll be interested to have your reaction to these. I myself find these statements difficult to accept, even allowing for the known rampant paranoia of Herod. But they were both quite adamant about the massacre.

Whatever the truth of the matter, it's not our pigeon. I won't be sorry to get out of here. Bethlehem is a haunted town.

Yours,

Gregory.

IMPERIAL PHYSICS LABORATORY

Project...23......

INVESTIGATION INTO REPORTED UFO SIGHTING, BETHLEHEM, ISRAEL

1. DATA MADE AVAILABLE BY GOVERNMENT OF ISRAEL (DEPARTMENT OF ECOLOGY)

1. On the night of December 24 a bright light, travelling slowly in the sky, approached Bethlehem from the east.

2. It was observed to hover over the Shepherds Fields (map ref. C2) descending rapidly to within two hundred feet of the ground.

3. It stayed in this position for about eight minutes during which time it emitted high-pitched sounds described as being like electronic music.

4. Some observers claim that they heard voices or a voice, but this is not officially accepted, the observers in question being superstitious peasants with no scientific training.

5. The object or light then disappeared completely.

6. Subsequently an outbreak of radiation sickness swept through the town causing the deaths of all male children under the age of two years. Adults and female children were not affected.

7. On the orders of the Medical Officer (Veterinary) in the Department of Agriculture (Jerusalem) the entire flock of sheep pastured in the affected area has been destroyed and the carcasses burned.

IMPERIAL PHYSICS LABORATORY

2. | PHYSICAL SURVEY

1. A detailed survey of the Shepherds Fields was carried out.

2. No trace of radio-activity was found. New grass is beginning to shoot through the winter growth (which is itself perfectly healthy and uncontaminated).

3. Soil samples, taken over a wide area, yielded no evidence of radiation burns.

4. Geiger counter readings in the houses where the children died were in every instance negative.

5. Clothing belonging to the dead children carried no trace of radio-active material.

3. | CONCLUSIONS

1. On the basis of the above survey there is no evidence to support the claim that a radio-active, extra-terrestrial body made a close approach to earth in the vicinity of Bethlehem on the night stated.

2. Since the bodies of the children affected have been cremated and the carcases of the sheep incinerated it is impossible to establish the nature of the sickness which is said to have killed them.

3. In the opinion of the investigating team there is no residual radio-active contamination in this locality (if indeed, there ever were).

Signed:

G.Patros. MSc.
Field Officer in Charge.

APPENDIX. PRIVATE AND CONFIDENTIAL.

Summary of interviews conducted by G. Patros

1. ## SUBJECT: MALE, JEWISH. AGE: 60+

   Subject, who refused to give his name, stated that five truck-
   loads of infantry drove into Bethlehem at dusk on January 3.
   The soldiers dispersed through the town, carried out a system-
   atic, house-to-house search and killed every male child under
   the age of two years. The bodies were taken in the trucks to
   the Jerusalem cemetery for immediate cremation.

2. ## SUBJECT: FEMALE, JEWISH. AGE: 31

   Subject independently corroborated 1st subject's story. She
   claimed to be the mother of one of the children killed by the
   soldiers. She described the massacre in detail with a kind of
   stunned calm.

3. Whilst it is difficult to imagine so barbarous an act as the
   deliberate butchering of children, the total absence of any
   evidence of radiation poisoning does raise certain questions -
   questions which will probably never be answered.

4. Although I attempted to interview several other citizens I was
   unsuccessful. My feeling is that there is a conspiracy of
   silence brought about by the threat of further reprisals. But
   reprisals for what?

    G.P.

PHOTOSTAT OF ENTRIES 18/24 IN THE IMMIGRATION RECORDS HELD AT
H.I.M. CUSTOMS CHECKPOINT, BEER SHEBA, SINAI.

7/

H.I.M. CUSTOMS   5 JUN 56

Zone SINAI   Checkpoint BEER SHEBA

Entry No.	Name	Sex	Age	Occupation	Destination	
18	DAVIDSON JOSEPH	M	37	CARPENTER	NAZARETH	✓
19	DAVIDSON MARY	F	28	HOUSEWIFE	NAZARETH	✓
20	DAVIDSON JESUS	M	8	—	NAZARETH	✓
21	COHEN GEDDY	M	54	PRIEST	JERUSALEM	✓
22	LEVITI SARAH	F	24	SECRETARY	TIBERIAS	✓
23	LEVY JOHN	M	32	AGRICULTURAL ENGINEER	SAMARIA	✓
24	DIMITRI ALEXANDRA	M	25	STUDENT	TIBERIAS	JS

DEPARTMENT
OF INTERNAL
· SECURITY ·

This marks the return of the Davidson family from
self-imposed exile in Egypt following the death
of Herod — and the beginning of all our
troubles!

G.

3 TEMPLE COURT   JERUSALEM   E2

Tel. 4224

14.4.60

Colonel Balthus Mezzeran,
Imperial Military College,
Tripoli.

My dear Balthus,

How nice to hear from you.   You lead a far more
exciting life than I, I'm afraid.   We jog along very
placidly here and I have nothing exciting to report.
Our days are filled with the familiar and we all know
what familiarity breeds.   Wait a minute, though - we
did have a surprise last week.   I doubt if it will seem
of much moment to you, though.   A soldier's surprises
are of a different calibre from those which stir a priest.
Still, it may interest you mildly.

We had just finished with our Passover Festival -
one of our busiest times here in the Temple.   The city
fills up with pilgrims (and tourists) and we're kept hard
at it with prayers and special services for the better
part of a week.   Anyway, it was over.   The crowds had
packed up and gone home and a few of us were sitting in
the Court of the Rabbis, relaxing over a glass of wine,
glad to have a bit of peace to talk together again.
Much as I imagine you must do in the Mess when you have seen
a course of cadets graduate.

Inevitably we were talking shop.   I'm afraid we all
have one-track minds in this profession.   I won't burden
you with the details (theology is fascinating only to
theologians) but we were all rather taken aback when a
twelve-year-old boy suddenly walked in, sat down and began
to ask questions.   The Chief Rabbi was in the chair and
with several of our most distinguished scholars present
the conversation was distinctly esoteric.   But this boy -
a carpenter's son from Nazareth with a patched shirt and
worn leather sandals and a Galilean accent you could hang
your hat on - this boy sailed in without an atom of self-
consciousness and began to put us right.

One of my colleagues - a rather fierce old gentleman,

actually - scowled at the lad and said, 'Off you go, son.
This is no place for children.'   And the boy looked at
him with genuine surprise and said, 'Why not, sir?   It is
my Father's house, isn't it?'

I know.   It sounds awful.   Pert.   Cheeky.   The
original precocious child at his unpleasant worst.   But
oddly enough it was not like that at all.   There was something about him - an openness, a kind of charisma - which
robbed his words of any offence.

The Chief Rabbi said, 'Quite right, son.   This is the
Father's house.'   And then his voice sharpened and he added,
'And we are discussing the Father's affairs.'   Which ought
to have shut the boy up, but didn't.   He smiled and said,
'Oh, good.   I'd like to join in, please.'

And that, astonishingly, is what he proceeded to do.
Quite brilliantly.   We found ourselves listening to him
spellbound, intrigued by his reasoning, astonished by the
depth of his knowledge.   I mean, it was heavy stuff, you
see.   The real doctrine.   But he had it all off pat.   The
Law and the Prophets, Torah and commentary, chapter and verse.
Magnificent.   For more than an hour he held us enthralled,
asking questions we could not begin to answer and then quietly
explaining them to us.   And all with such charm, such genuine,
unspoiled enthusiasm.   Even in a grown man with years of
scholarship behimd him, it would have been a superlative
performance.   But from a boy of twelve it was - well, phenomenal.

As one of the scribes said to me afterwards, 'He was saying
things I've always wanted to say and could never find the words
to express.'   I agreed.

I really think we would have stayed there all day listening to him, questioning him and - yes - I admit it, learning
from him.   Some of his ideas were extremely daring.   Rash,
almost.   And yet always contained within a framework of logic.
Marvellous.

But then his mother arrived in a flutter of anxiety.
They had apparently been on their way home to Nazareth with a
party of friends when they found the boy missing.   Not a
pleasant experience.   They had come rushing back to Jerusalem
in a panic to find him.   She was a decent, modest woman.
Quite pretty in a countryish sort of way.   But very ordinary.

And terribly embarrassed of course.   I'm afraid we make quite
a formidable assembly even off-duty.   She rushed up to the
boy and took his arm.   'Oh, Jesus,' she said.   'There you
are.   We've been so worried about you.   Looked everywhere
for you.'   It was obvious that she was very distressed and I
thought the boy would be crestfallen.   But not a bit of it.
'You worry too much, Mother,' he said, firmly, you understand,
but not unkindly.   'You might have known I'd be here in my
Father's house.'

And that was odd, because he said it as though he meant
it literally.   The house of my Father.   But, as I mentioned,
his father is a carpenter.   I mean, we all use the expression
'in the Father's house' for the Temple.   But this boy - it
wasn't like that with him.   It was - well, an accurate, literal
description.   He thinks God is his Father.   Or, put another
way - he thinks he is God's son - the Son of God.

That might not mean very much to you, my dear old pagan
friend.   But to us it means something very special - very
important.   To us it means, in a word, Messiah.   The God-King
for whom we wait.   The Liberator of Israel.   Over the years
many men have appeared in our history claiming to be Messiah.
But I can find no record of anyone making such a claim at the
age of twelve.

His mother began to apologise to the Chief Rabbi but the
boy interrupted her.   'Don't apologise, Mother,' he said.
'There's no need.   We have been discussing my Father's affairs.'
And he smiled at us - that charming, innocent, strangely wise
smile that lighted up his dark eyes and gave his face a kind
of, well, radiance, I suppose is the word.   And he said to
her, 'After all, that's why I'm here, isn't it?'

And once again, Balthus, I had that odd feeling.   A kind
of premonition, a shiver of expectancy.   For so will Messiah
speak when he comes, and with the same authority and grace.

But a twelve-year-old boy?   How can that be?

His mother called him Jesus.   A common enough name among
us, of course.   And the sort of name Messiah might take.
Jesus.   It means 'One who saves'.

Sarah says I'm imagining things.   She says the Passover
took too much out of me this year and I ought to think seriously

about retiring to a country parish. She's probably right. I'm getting old and tired. And, do you know, for the first time I find myself regretting my years. Because I doubt if I'll still be here when that boy grows up and declares himself. As I feel in my bones he will. To be there when he enters the Temple a grown man and makes himself known to us as Messiah - that would be something. That would be really something.

Well, well. Perhaps Sarah is right. Perhaps it's all in my imagination. And yet, the others who were there with me, they also were astounded - disturbed, even. Whoever the boy is, he's got a great future. We're all agreed on that.

Forgive me, I've rambled on too long about this. You'll be impatient with an old man's musings. But we get so little excitement here. When something like this happens we tend to magnify it, I'm afraid. Wishful thinking, perhaps. At every Passover we say the same thing: 'Next year Messiah will come.'

My greetings to your wife,

Yours,

Heliopolis House Hotel

Heliopolis, Egypt
Tel: Heliopolis 644

15th March '78

The Manager,
Trekker Tours (Rome) Ltd,
31/33 Via Flavia,
Rome.

Dear Victor,

Your telex came in this morning. I will take the
Nile Valley trip as per your request before returning to
Head Office.

You'll see from my report (sent yesterday, airmail)
that I've done a pretty exhaustive survey of the Syria-
Israel-Sinai-Lower Egypt safari route. It's all looking
good to me and I recommend we press on now with the
literature as scheduled. Our new-style package/percentage
deal has gone down well with the hoteliers and I think we
can expect a lot of satisfied customers. For the rest,
it's been the usual: too many flies and too much dust -
you know what the Middle East is like. I suppose the first
time you see it there's a certain glamour, but I've been
this way too many times to drool over it now. For my
money it's pretty boring except occasionally when something

odd crops up. Like it did a couple of days ago, actually.

We'd come down the west shore of the Dead Sea that
morning, heading south into Sinai to check the road con-
ditions into Eilat (better than I'd dared to hope. See
pp 6/7 in my report) and we were well and truly out in the
blue when we broke a half-shaft. The driver carries a
full kit of spares (as per our advertisement) so there was
no real panic, just a question of killing a couple of hours,
miles from anywhere in a waste of rock and sand and a
temperature of 115 plus. Not exactly a load of laughs,
but it could've been worse.

There was a wadi just off the road and I walked down
it about half a mile. Wadis and churches - when you've
seen one you've seen 'em all - and I was just about to
turn back when I saw him, or rather heard him, you know
how quiet it can be in the desert. There was this rock-
fall banked up the side of the wadi and I heard this
curious sound coming from round behind it. A sort of
chant, it was. Groups of words repeated over and over
again in sing-song voice. Very weird. As you know, I'm
into soul music but this was really spaced-out stuff. I
edged my way carefully round the foot of the rocks and
saw him crouching on the sand with his back to me,
chanting away like a junkie on horse. All in Hebrew, of
course, so most of it was over my head, but I picked out
the odd word here and there and made some sort of sense
of it. 'All the poor people,' he was chanting. 'All
the hungry people. Hungry for hope. Hungry for love.'
And every now and then he'd lash out with his fists and

shout, 'Get away, Shaitan, get away from me.' I checked it out later and find Shaitan is the Hebrew name for the devil.

Hullo, I thought, we've got a right one here. He was in a pretty sorry state, ragged clothes and hair down to his shoulders and his feet bare and filthy with dust and sand, badly scratched and a few deep cuts. It's pretty stony down there, you see, and hellish desolate and he looked like he'd been there quite some time.

I went a bit closer and said, 'Shalom, friend,' and he whipped round and leapt to his feet. 'Away,' he shouted. 'Get away from me. 1'm not hungry. I don't want your bread.' Just a young chap, late twenties, hair all over his face, a great black beard clogged with sweat and sand. And woefully thin, hollow-cheeked and his eyes like coals sunk deep in his head. I made sympathetic noises to try to calm him down a bit. He seemed - well, not angry exactly - more wild, intense. Even a bit frightened, as if I were some sort of threat to him. It was like an oven down there on the wadi floor and the sweat was pouring out of him. I said, 'Look, let's get up a bit higher. There's a breeze blowing across those rocks up there, cool you down a bit.' I took a couple of steps towards him but he backed off, turned and went up those rocks like a mountain goat, sat down on the top and glared at me. I followed him up carefully, taking my time so as not to spook him, and eventually sat down about two yards away. He turned his back on me and stared out over the desert. It's pretty flat round there and you can see half Sinai if you get high enough. After a moment or two he looked at me

fiercely and started muttering and shouting again,
something about it not being mine to give him, which
didn't make a lot of sense to me. I shook my head and
smiled. 'It's OK, old chap,' I said, or something
similar. You know, the usual bromides just to occupy
his mind a bit. I mean, he was way and gone, really out
in hyper-space somewhere. I reached out to touch him,
give him a pat on the shoulder like you would a frightened
dog, but he shot up and stood there balanced on top of the
rocks. 'Easy,' I said. 'Easy, pal.' And off he went
again, muttering and weaving. Seemed to think I was going
to push him off or something. I reckoned one wrong word
and he'd chuck himself down and do himself a considerable
mischief. So I sat tight for a bit and let him settle.
He crouched down then, his head in his hands, his eyes
watching me through his fingers, like a caged animal he
was. Really over the top.

We stayed like that for about a quarter of an hour
I suppose. Every time I tried to get through to him he
pushed his arms out, spread his hands and shouted for me
to get away. Which in the end is what I did. I was
obviously doing him no good anyway, so I climbed back
down to the wadi floor and he sat up there and watched me
like a great, ragged bird, watching a mouse. I pointed
back the way I'd come and shouted up to him that there'd
be food and water by the road any time he liked to come
and get it. And then I walked off and left him.

When I got back to the car, the driver was just
putting the wheel back on, all axle-grease and drenched in
sweat. We sat down in the shade of the car and had some

coffee and a bite to eat and I told them about the poor
guy up the wadi. The driver shrugged and said it was
probably a holy man - a prophet, he called him - doing
his statutory tour of fasting and prayer. I said I
thought he was in a pretty bad way and might well not last
much longer, but the driver just grinned and said they
could go for weeks sometimes living off their fat. I said
this guy didn't have too much fat to live off and was
hallucinating in the wildest possible way and needed care
and attention. But the driver said no way would he let
us help him. These holy boys are fanatically independent,
apparently. Masochistic, too. So in the end we packed
up and pushed on, leaving a loaf and a small bottle of
water by the road. I insisted on that. It wasn't much
and he probably never came to find it, but I felt better
just leaving it in case.

Well, that's it, Victor. I don't suppose it's the
sort of thing we can put in the brochures. 'Breakfast
in Jerusalem, two hours to explore the Old City and then
off to Eilat for a swim, with a ten minute break en route
to throw a crumb or two to the local fakir.' I don't
somehow think the punters would go a bundle on that.
Funny, though, I keep thinking about him out there on his
own with only the flies and his personal ghosts for
company. I wonder what it's all in aid of, really? What
he hopes to gain from it? One thing, if he survives, the
rest of his life'll be a cake-walk after that. Perhaps
that's the idea. A taste of hell before you start,
instead of waiting till you die like the rest of us.

9/6

Ah well, it takes all sorts. I'll probably ring you
from Luxor. Reversed charges, naturally.

See you next week,

Vince

10/,

14 The Crescent,
Cana,
Galilee.
10 th March '79

Dear Becky,

I thought you'd like to hear about Susan Goldings wedding last week (you remember Susan, pretty little thing, her father runs the bank opposite the Church). Between you and me, dear, she was just in time. Don't misunderstand me, she wasn't pregnant or anything like that, but she is twenty-four and just a shade on the plump side and she takes after her mother, which means that by the time she's thirty she's going to be huge, so it was now or never, if you see what I mean?

The boy's quite nice (if you go for the machismo type) with a black moustache and a pair of shoulders you could block a road with. And of course there's a fair bit of money there, his people are in shipping and own half the Haifa docks I believe, which can't be bad can it? So what with the bank and the big boats it was quite a wedding, just about every-body in the town was there plus a good sprinkling of farming gentry (the Range Rover Brigade as Jim calls them). It was all just a bit too too (if you know what I mean) but the food was marvellous. I mean the ceremony in the church was lovely, of course, but a wedding stands or falls on the Reception doesn't it, and they certainly did us proud. They hired a marquee and had it set up on the lawn behind the house. Cana is very pretty at this time of the year and it was a lovely day (happy the bride the sun shines on) for it. Susan looked the part to perfection in white lace and a full train, with four bridesmaids and two pages!! It must have cost them a bomb, still it's once in a lifetime, isn't it? Hopefully, anyway!

I said everybody was there and I meant it. I mean, would you believe the Davidsons from Nazareth!! You can't cast the net much wider than that can you, dear? Joe Davidson's dead, of course. Heart, I think it was, about three years ago. His eldest son Jesus took over the business for a while, did quite well I believe. So it was a bit of a surprise when he walked out earlier this year and left his brothers to get on with it. Got religion you see, took it into his head to be a - y'know - itinerant preacher. Itinerant scrounger more like because he doesn't work at all now, just traipses around with this bunch of followers and very odd some of them are, too. The Zebedee boys, for instance, and the Johnson brothers - Simon and Andrew. Andrew's all right I suppose but that Simon, honestly, all black beard and horse teeth, horse laugh too !! Oh yes, dear, he brought them along, he takes them everywhere, y'know. And his poor little mother, she's lost a lot of weight since her husband died, not surprising really with all the worry she's had about Jesus.

They were all bunched together at the end of the table and Mary Davidson in the middle with that odious little tax-man, Matthew Levison, on one side and a thin, beetle-browed man called Judas Iscariot on the other.

They say Jesus is beginning to make a name for himself because apparently he's not a bad speaker (considering his origins) and the ordinary, run-of-the-mill peasants seem to like him, perhaps because he talks their language and seems to share their rather sly sense of humour, always making jokes at the expense of respectable citizens (you know how they do). It must be very embarrassing for his mother, she's such a quiet little thing. Dotes on Jesus, of course, heaven only knows why considering how he's treated her, but she does. Hangs on every word he says.

Anyway, the wedding. There we all were enjoying ourselves, plenty to eat and plenty to drink (Abe Golding keeps an excellent cellar, being something of a connoisseur - if that's how you spell it) and then this awful thing happened, the wine ran out!! Awful? It was a disaster!! I mean, can you imagine how Hannah Golding felt? They'd hired extra domestic staff for the

day (with a real butler, would you believe) and everything was going smoothly until the butler (an impressive
figure but his finger nails could have been cleaner)
bent over Abe Golding's chair and said something in
his ear. Abe looked at his wife and her face went
very pale and sort of crumpled up. It was quite funny
really, in an awful sort of way, her sitting there
like a queen at her only daughter's wedding, no
expense spared, everybody who was anybody packed
into that marquee, the tables groaning with food —
and suddenly, in the middle of it all, nothing to
drink! I knew exactly what she was thinking, dear,
her social reputation ruined, all her airs and graces
exposed, no longer that well-bred banker's wife whose
daughter made such a good marriage, just the woman
who couldn't even manage a wedding breakfast and
get it right! Too embarrassing, dear!!
　　Her eyes flickered round the table from face to face.
I thought: any second now, my girl, you're either going
to faint or have hysterics. And it sort of communicated
itself. Everybody stopped talking and sat staring at her
silently. And then Mary Davidson spoke to that son of
hers. "Can you do something, Jesus?" she said. "Please!"
　　Jesus didn't look too pleased. He said, rather curtly,
"You don't understand, woman. It's not time yet." They
say he's like that, talks in riddles half the time, but
the way he does it, dear, so hard, so ill-mannered.
Dreadful!! I expected her to curl up and cry, I know

I would have in her place, but she didn't. She looked up at the butler and smiled. "Just do whatever he tells you", she said.

Jesus looked at her, his face set. There was something strange about him, a kind of — oh, I can't describe it but it made me shiver just to watch him! Then he said to the butler, "Have you got any water?" And somebody laughed, because it was such an anti-climax! Not that he seemed in the least bothered. He was talking to the butler again, quite calm now, quite relaxed, and the butler nodded, and pointed to six enormous water jars — y'know, dear, those big porous coolers we still use up here, primitive but very effective. Anyway, the butler called up some of the waiters and they went to the jars and started ladling water into jugs.

Becky, I don't know how to tell you this, only it wasn't water, you see! Oh it was water in the coolers but when they put the jugs on the table it was wine, and very good wine, too!!

How did Jesus do it? I don't know, dear, I honestly don't know. Of course there'll be no holding the man now. The whole district's buzzing with the story and everytime he appears in a village the crowds come from miles around just to see and hear him. Mind you, it won't last. He's heading for trouble and fast, getting very political so they say. He'll come to a bad end, I'm afraid; born to be hanged, as they say.

It's his mother I feel sorry for, poor love, I mean, Jesus can take his chance but she's the one who's going to suffer in the end. One of these days she's going to look back at that wedding and wish she'd kept her mouth shut.

Well, I've gossipped on long enough, but I thought you'd be interested. Take care now.
Love,
Miriam

Hardly the sort of conjuring trick from the Messiah
G.

Rabbi Ezra Shobach,   18th April '79
4b Temple Mews,
Jerusalem.

My dear Ezra,

This is, I'm afraid, a good news, bad news letter. And one that will almost certainly disappoint you.

First, the good news. I have spoken at some length with Jesus Davidson. We met last night in the roof garden of the house in Bethany where he is currently staying. I was able to make the journey unobserved. Nor was I followed on the way home. So far, so good.

The bad news is that I very much doubt he is your man. I believe him to be a good man, possessed of astonishing insight, especially considering his background and upbringing, and well-versed in the Law and the Prophets. His conversation is both intelligent and far-seeing, but he is curiously evasive when it comes to practical issues. As a talker and a thinker he is quite outstanding. As a man of action, I doubt if he will fulfil your expectations. I put him down as being an idealist - a dreamer even - not a revolutionary.

I must confess I am myself relieved to find him so. As you are well aware I have never been entirely happy about the methods you propose to employ to achieve our ends. A warrior Messiah bent on the destruction of Roman power by violent action - this is a concept I cannot fully accept. And certainly, in Jesus Davidson, we have no such Messiah. He is deeply non-violent in his attitudes, and his thinking about Messiah is of such complexity that it makes your hopes of a sort of holy war seem simplistic.

We have been conditioned to think of the Day of the Lord - the advent and triumph of Messiah - in terms of military action; to defeat the occupying forces of Rome by armed insurrection. But Jesus rejects this completely. He speaks of the Day of the Lord (which he calls the coming of the Kingdom) as being a day of liberty, yes. But liberty not only for us but for all men. A liberty only to be realised as we learn to love our enemies and wish for them not death but a new birth. Only by being born again, he says, can we enter God's Kingdom.

In the hope of drawing him out on this idea I pretended to take it literally and asked him how an old man like myself could enter again into the physical process of birth. He looked at me with a kind of amusement. He has brilliant, very dark eyes which seem to penetrate any defence. I knew then he understood my rather naive ploy. He asked me about baptism and we spoke for a little while about John and his baptising in Jordan. Then he said, 'But there is a greater baptism than this. There is the baptism of the Spirit of God.' And he said that this was the true baptism. And the true freedom. 'You must be born again,' he said (again that curious phrase), 'by the power of the Spirit.'

I really didn't follow this and said so. He looked surprised. 'You,' he said, 'a leading theologian in Israel - you don't understand this?' I shook my head, feeling a little uncomfortable. He has a way of pinning you down with that look of his. 'If you don't believe me when I speak of the things of this life,' he said then, 'how can you begin to believe when I speak of the Kingdom?'

I suppose I should have felt insulted. A carpenter's son talking to me in that way. But I didn't. Only confused. As if I were on the brink of a whole new dimension of faith and couldn't find the way into it.

I won't bore you with the rest of our conversation. Enough to say that I was groping after him and he was miles ahead of me, moving with an ease of thought through what to me were very profound and puzzling depths indeed. But finally I said that I doubted we could win our freedom without recourse to suffering and death. And he agreed whole-heartedly. 'That is why Messiah has come to you,' he said. 'To suffer and die so that you may have life. Any man who believes in him will inherit eternal life.'

I asked him who this Messiah was and he looked at me steadily for a long moment. 'Do you really have to ask that?' he said then. 'Do you not know who I am, Nicodemus?'

Ezra, I'm not sure. Not one hundred per cent sure, you understand? But I think he is Messiah. I think he is the one for whom we have waited so long. I think in him we shall find our freedom. But how is another matter. Certainly not your way. He clearly foresees himself as dying for Israel - indeed, for the world. But what kind of Messiah is this who brings death upon himself rather than upon his enemies? And how can Messiah - as we have been taught to know him and recognise him - how can he ever die?

These questions haunt me, turning like knives in my head. If Jesus is to be believed, we will have to re-think our entire theology of the Kingdom, re-structure our strategy, assume attitudes we have always rejected as being valueless. And above all, Ezra, we shall have to learn to believe in the power of love to suffer and die and somehow triumph.

None of which, I imagine, will appeal to you and the others who think as you do. Which is why I say Jesus is not your man. Not yours nor mine nor anyone's. He is his own man and that is his strength. If he truly is Messiah, we shall never bend him to our ways. Rather we shall have to adjust to his. I doubt you will want to consider doing that. I'm not at all sure I do.

One thing is sure, you are right about Caiaphas hating him. I think Jesus is aware of that, and quite unmoved by it. He as good as told me that, in the end, Caiaphas would sacrifice him, using the safety of the realm as his excuse. He said that Caiaphas, acting from all the wrong motives, would in fact become an instrument of God, enabling the Son of Man (which is his favourite title for himself, and as you know a Messianic one) to fulfil his destiny and die for the world of men.

Which again is a complex concept which makes your straightforward

4

conflict between good and evil simplistic. Perhaps it is. We have,
after all, a history of valiant men who have fought bravely against
great odds to free the people from their oppressors. All have done
well in their time - but all have failed. Violence is, in the end,
self-destructive. Only some positive force can hope to break the
vicious circle. Is that force love?

You will be impatient with this kind of surmising. You are a
man of action and like things to be expressed clearly in pragmatic
terms. But Jesus has a much more subtle understanding of the issues.
I cannot at this stage say that I fully understand or support his
thinking. But I am fascinated by it and intend to pursue the thoughts
he has planted in my mind.

You, of course, will look elsewhere for your warrior-king.
Perhaps this Jesus Barabbas is your man, as Jesus Davidson assuredly
is not. But if he is Messiah, and if he dies ... Ezra, if God dies,
what is there left for us to hope for, in this life or the next?

Well, I have done as you asked - interviewed Jesus Davidson in
the hope that he is the one we expect. I am bound to tell you he
is not - not the one we expect. But whether or not he is the One
who shall come - the One we ought to expect - this I cannot answer.
Not yet.

Yours
Nicodemus

Whilst I have never had a great deal of Time for
Nicodemus it is nonetheless disturbing to note this
early attempt on the part of Davidson to corrupt
the Sanhedrin

G.

Xth LEGION

THE IMPERIAL ROMAN ARMY

J.W.

APO Box 25/B18 MEF

POSTAL SURVEILLANCE DEPT — ISS STATE SECURITY P — 9.4.79

My dearest Flavia,

A rather extraordinary thing has happened. You remember
Marcus, my batman? Tall, thin chap with glasses. Looks like
a bank manager. Talks like one, too. Very calm and matter
of fact. Been with me four years now and never put a foot
wrong.

Well, this morning he was dying. He didn't come in with
my shaving water, the way he always does, and I went through
and found him on the floor by his bed. He was in a terrible
state - sweating and shivering, delirious with fever, his face
blanco-white, scum on his lips, his eyes sunk right down into
his head.

I got him up on the bed a put a couple of blankets over
him - he was cold as ice except for his forehead which was
burning - and went down to the mess to get the M.O. He came
back with me straightaway and had a good look at Marcus. I
said 'What's the verdict?' He shook his head and shrugged.
Apparently it was some sort of virus and the M.O. had nothing
to touch it. 'Seen it before, Cass,' he said, 'a couple of
times. All we can do is let it take its course.' I said, 'But
good God, man, he's dying.' The M.O. nodded. 'Sorry, Cass,'
he said, 'There's nothing I can do. Keep him warm and wait.
Maybe he'll get lucky.'

By breakfast-time it was all over the unit - you know
how fast news travels in the army - especially bad news. The
adjutant stopped me in the doorway of the Mess and said he
was sorry and why didn't I try the Healer? The Healer is a
Jew - a local man. Ran a small joinery business with his
father and then jacked it all in and went off round the
country healing people - or claiming to, anyway. I didn't
fancy his chances much. If our M.O. was stumped I didn't
see the local witch-doctor getting very far. The adjutant

said 'Worth a try, Cass. He's said to be spot on-with fevers.'

I went back up to the billet to have another look at
Marcus. He was obviously worse. Much worse. The fever was eating
him alive and it didn't look to me as though he'd last the day.
So I thought, 'Hell, man what've you got to lose?' and went to
find the Healer.

Which wasn't all that difficult. He was in the next village
with a big crowd round him. My first thought was if this was
his normal morning surgery he had to be better than average.
You don't pull a crowd like that unless you're on target at
least 70% of the time. I stood and watched him for a minute
or two, sizing him up a bit. I must say he impressed me even
then. Big chap. Good shoulders. Straight back. Bearded of
course. Hair down to his shoulders. But that's normal out
here. They all look like drop-outs. What I liked about him
was his composure, his authority. He was in control of the
situation, you see. And that's not easy in a street full of
beggers and traders. Women yacketting away in their shrill
Jewish voices. Kids milling round screaming their heads off,
Flies. Dust. General chaos.

Anyway, I pushed my may through to him, saluted and told
him the story. 'I'm in the army, sir,' I said. God knows why.
I mean, I was in full rig-of-the-day - denims, jump boots,
beret, side arms. Telling him I was a soldier was a touch
superfluous. But it showed how uptight I was over Marcus.
'And I like to do things the army way,' I said. 'I get my
orders and I give my orders. Obey and expect to be obeyed.
Chain of command, y'see. I imagine it's much the same with
you, sir?' He smiled and nodded, half-amused, half-sympathetic.
'What d'you want me to do, Captain?' he said.

I said, 'I can see how busy you are. And blood's thicker
than water. I'm a Roman. You're a Jew. But my batman's pretty
well done for.' He said, 'So?' I said 'So if you'll just give
the order - say the word - and heal him. Please.'

I don't mind telling you, love, I was sweating. I mean,
there must be a drill for that sort of thing. Prayers.
Incantations - that sort of mumbo-jumbo. But he said, 'You
really think that's all there is to it? I just say the word
and your man's healed?' He was staring at me. Big,dark eyes,
very steady, very - well, penetrating. God I thought, I'm
making a fist of this. Proper dog's breakfast. But I remembered
poor old Marcus sweating his life away back in the billet.
So I stood up to him. Met his eyes firmly and said , 'Yes,
sir. Yes, I do,' and y'know, love, the odd thing was, I did.
At that precise moment I really believed he could swing it
for Marcus.

He looked at me for a moment or two - but it seemed like
bloody hours - and then he smiled and turned to the crowd.
'Now then, you people.' he said. 'This is the real thing. This
is what I'm looking for in Israel. A man who believes in me.'
I felt a complete idiot, stuck there in the middle of the street
with the sweat running down my back under my shirt and everybody
gawping at me. Then he turned back to me and said, 'Don't w
worry any more, Captain. Your man's all right now.'

I saluted and backed-off and had a quick look at my watch.
11.00 hours. All the way back to the billet I was in a kind
of vacuum - not daring to hope. Not daring to disbelieve
either. Sort of balanced. On a knife-edge between relief and
despair. Odd sort of feeling. I can't really describe it. But
it took a couple of years off my life.

When I got back, there was Marcus standing in the doorway
of the billet, waiting for me with a mug of coffee in his hand.
He looked marvellous. All bright-eyed and bushy-tailed.
Grinning from ear to ear, his glasses glinting in the sunlight.

I grinned back. 'So,' I said. 'It was just malingering,
was it? A touch of the old soldiers?' I took the mug of coffee
from him and drank a couple of mouthfuls. 'All right now?'
I said. He nodded. 'Yes, sir. Thank you. Quite OK.' I said,
'Good man.' And then, casually - or as casually as I could
manange - 'Since when?' And he said, 'Eleven o'clock, sir.'

So there you are. I don't know how the Healer did it,
and I don't much care. The M.O. says it's a miracle. Which
it is, I suppose. Marcus is fit again. That's the main thing.
As he said just now when he brought in my Mess kit for dinner,
'Somebody up there loves me, sir.' I think that says it all.

Take care of yourself, love.

Cassius
x

a coincidence? these army doctors
have never impressed me

G,

13/1

CUTTING FROM
THE SOUTH GALILEE NEWS
27.5.79

Jaffa Syl...
1.30 p.m. No flowers by req...
donations to Jaffa Epilepsy Research
Centre.

GIAH. On 23.5.79 peacefully at her
home, Rachael, beloved wife of
Solomon Giah, in her 52nd year.
Private funeral. No flowers.

ISAACSON. On 25.5.79 in the
Cottage Hospital Nain, after a long
illness bravely borne, Peter James,
23, only son of Salome and the late
Benjamin Isaacson. Funeral 11 a.m.
Thursday at the Nain synagogue.
Flowers to A.T. Simons & Son, F.D.,
High Street, Nain. Telephone Nain
532.

MACHIR. On 24.5.79 suddenly, on
his farm at Nablus, Jeremish, husband
of Rebb... father of Ruth and

Resurrection or Recovery? Coroner to Decide

In the Nazareth Crown Court next Tuesday, Mr Reuben Adams, the District Coroner, will be asked to give a ruling on the official status of a dead man who was brought back to life on the day of his funeral.

Mr Peter James Isaacson of 4 Hillside Terrace, Nain, a patient in the Nain Cottage Hospital, was certified dead on the 25th of last month. The certificate was signed by Dr Matthew Zachar, the Senior Registrar. The cause of death was leukaemia.

But at the funeral last Thursday morning the cortege was halted on its way to the cemetery by Jesus Davidson, the revolutionary young prophet from Nazareth who is widely believed to have powers of healing. In spite of protests from the rabbi and the shocked mourners, Davidson had the coffin opened. He then took the dead man by the hand, brought him back to life and gave him to his mother.

Interviewed yesterday by our reporter, Rabbi Amos Yacoub said, 'It is all most unfortunate. The young man was in a deep coma and should never have been brought to me for burial. We can only be grateful that the mistake was discovered in time.'

But Dr Zachar rejects this explanation. He is adamant that no mistake was made by the hospital. 'We have a properly laid-down procedure to establish the fact of death,' he said. 'All the tests were positive. This was not a coma.'

Working happily with her son in the garden of 4 Hillside Terrace, Mrs Isaacson said, 'Of course Peter was dead. Everybody knows that.' Asked how she thought Davidson had brought her son back to life, she said, 'I don't know how. You'll have to ask him that.' But, as usual, Davidson was not available for comment.

What is quite certain is that Peter Isaacson is alive today. Was it simply a remarkable recovery? Or was it a resurrection? This is the question the Coroner must answer on Tuesday.

CUTTING FROM THE SOUTH GALILEE NEWS 3.6.79

An emotional charade in the worst possible taste. Typical Davidson
G.

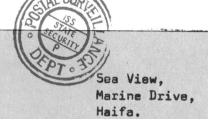

Sea View,
Marine Drive,
Haifa.

6 February '81

John darling,

This is a very difficult letter to write. I wanted to
come up to Capernaum myself and see you and tell you what's
happened. But Daddy won't hear of it. Perhaps he's right.
It might, as he says, be traumatic for both of us to meet
again.

Oh, darling, I don't know how to say this without hurting
you dreadfully, but - well, I can't marry you. I want to.
I want to more than anything else in the world. But I can't.
My parents have forbidden it and, of course I'm still under-
age and need their consent. And they won't give it, darling.
They just won't.

The thing is, they've found out. Daddy was up in Damascus
last week on a business trip and when he came back he and Mummy
went into a long huddle in his study. He looked very upset
when he came in and I thought it was something to do with his
work. But it wasn't, John. It was you - us!

Apparently he met a man from Capernaum in the hotel where
he was staying and they got talking. Daddy told him about
us - you know how much he's always admired you. 'My daughter's
engaged to a young fellow from your town,' he said, and mentioned
your name. It was really the worst kind of luck that this
man happened to be a pillar of the local church and knew all
about your meeting with Jesus Davidson. I gather he was one
of those who totally disapproved of the whole incident. And
he certainly filled Daddy in on the details.

Oh, darling, darling John, I'm so miserable! Mummy's
done her best to stand up for you, bless her. But by the time
Daddy had got through telling her about your illness and how

Jesus treated you - he can't even now bring himself to use
the word 'cure' - she was shocked and upset as he was. I
keep telling them you're perfectly well now - have been from
the moment Jesus spoke to you that day. But they've got it
into their heads - thanks to this odious man from the church
there - that there's something - oh, I hate even to write
it, darling - something abnormal about you. All Mummy can
say is, 'Think of the risk, dear. John may appear to be
healthy and everything. But you can never be sure, Naomi,'
she said. 'Even if he stays well, there's always the chance
any children might be affected.'

Daddy nodded. 'I know it's a big heart-break for you,
love,' he said. 'But better to face it now than later. Just
as well I ran into this chap when I did. Otherwise you could
have been married and none the wiser.'

Of course I told them I knew all about it - that you'd
told me about your illness and how you'd gone into the church
that morning, all bewildered and frightened, and shouted at
Jesus. Mummy was horrified. 'He shouted?' she said. 'In
church?' As if that was some sort of unforgiveable sin or
something. I pointed out to her - to both of them - it wasn't
really you who shouted. It was the illness affecting your
brain. And of course that started them off again, worse than
before. All 'I-told-you-so' and 'There-you-are-you-see!' Daddy
said the man he'd met had told him what a terrible scene
there'd been with everybody in the congregation horrified by
the things you were shouting out. So I said, 'And did he
also tell you how Jesus cured John? How he spoke a word and
the illness left him and they all began to praise God for a
miracle?' Daddy said well, yes, the man did mention that.
But not very convincingly. He told Daddy they'd all had doubts
about it lasting.

I said, 'But it has lasted. It's more than eighteen
months ago now and there's never been the slightest sign of
trouble.' I mean, they know that! Ever since you and I
started going out together a year ago, they've seen you often
enough. Liked you, too. But now - oh, I don't know. I've
argued and argued with them. But they won't listen any more.

Reading between the lines - and from something Mummy said - I think there's a bit more to it than just your illness, darling. As you know, Daddy's firm is hoping to land this big contract in Jerusalem. Something to do with church property I think, in the Temple precincts. They're all sitting with their fingers crossed waiting for the Temple authorities to sign on the dotted line. And Daddy's a bit jumpy in case anything goes wrong at the last minute. Apparently it's very much his responsibility to see the contract through, and he's scared they might change their minds or something.

And of course, Jesus is not very popular with the authorities. They don't like him. In fact, if Daddy is to be believed, they'd like to see him arrested and put on trial. I don't quite know what for. I mean, I've never met him, but from all you've told me about him, and from everything I hear, he's a really marvellous sort of person. Kind and understanding and able to do wonderful things for people. But they seem to think he's dangerous, heaven knows why.

Still, it doesn't help us much, you see. Daddy feels that if were to get around that his daughter is going to marry a man whom Jesus cured of insanity, then that would put paid to the contract and leave him in a very awkward situation with the directors of the firm. I suppose he's right to be worried. I just wish he'd be honest enough to come right out and say so instead of making all these ridiculous excuses about you not being - well normal.

Darling, what are we going to do? It's two more years yet before I come of age! I can't expect you to wait that long - and to be forbidden to see me or write to me or anything. Is it very wicked of me to wish you'd never met Jesus Davidson? To wish you'd seen a doctor and had some recognised psychiatric treatment to get you well again? But then I remember how you said you'd seen so many doctors and none of them had been able to help. And how Jesus changed your whole life in just a moment or two. And I couldn't wish for that not to have happened, darling. I couldn't wish that!

Oh, John I love you so much! And everything was so wonderful and happy and exciting. And now it's all such a mess. And so hopeless! I have to do what Mummy and Daddy say - you know that. But it's so cruel! So unnecessarily cruel to both of us.

You've told me so often that Jesus bases his whole life on loving people. That's what makes him so strong and able to work miracles and everything. But what about our love, John? Can your Jesus make that come true for us, in spite of everything that's happened? I wish I could believe that he could. But I can't. Not with Mummy weeping and Daddy snarling round the house, angry with himself as much as with you.

Please don't answer this. They won't let me read any letters you send. They say it has to be a clean break. That however much it hurts - and, oh darling, how it hurts - it's the only way to deal with the situation. They even say I'll thank them in the end, meet a nice, normal man (their words, not mine) and settle down happily with him!! As if I could ever look at anyone but you, darling.

I know you'll want to come down and see me - and them. Please don't! Mummy and I are going away for a little while. Egypt first and then on to Cyprus. Daddy has it all arranged. We leave tomorrow morning. The idea is to take my mind off you and help me to settle down afterwards. Oh, it's so stupid.

I can't write any more now. Try not to think too badly of me - of us. And, if it still means anything to you, I love you. I always will.

PS. It can't be right, though, can it? What Jesus says about love healing all wounds. Nobody could love you more than I do. But all that's happened is I've wounded you and myself. I'm so sorry, John darling. So very, very sorry.

A classic example of how Davidson disturbs and confuses all who come under his influence G.

ISRAELI POLICE headquarters

King David Sq
Jerusalem WI

Y DEPT

ROOM 401

TRANSCRIPT OF TELEPHONE CONVERSATION
RECORDED 15.03 Hours   DATE August 25 '79

CLASSIFICATION: SECRET

ORIGIN OF CALL: 031-63-495

ADDRESS: 24 Lakeside Drive, Decapolis, Galilee

CALLER'S NAME: Elizabeth Zenner (Mrs), Wife of Matthew Zenner, Mayor
                  of Decapolis.

CONNECTION: 015-28-9107

ADDRESS: 183 Nablus Avenue, Jerusalem NE2

RECEIVED BY: Anne Johnson (Mrs), Daughter of M Zenner, Wife of Mark
                  Johnson, Company Director, P T Johnson Ltd, Wine Merchant.

EXCERPT READS:

EZ: Jesus Davidson, would you believe?

AJ: Who? Oh yes, I know. The healer from Nazareth. Momma, how
      marvellous.

EZ: That's what your father thought. 'An honour for the town,' he said.

AJ: Well it was rather, wasn't it? I mean he's quite famous now and .....

EZ: Famous? Notorious, more like.

AJ: Oh, Momma, that's not fair. He's a good man. Everybody says so.
      Look at all the people he's .....

EZ: Darling, he's a nobody. A carpenter's son, yet.

AJ: Oh yes, but he's more than that, Momma. They say he .....

EZ: I don't care what they say, Anne. All I know is he's got no manners
      no respect for the common courtesies of life.

AJ: But surely what he's doing is .....

EZ: He insulted us, that's what he did. Deliberately insulted us -
       the town, your father, me, everybody. I've never been so
       humiliated in all my life. It was dreadful, dear. Quite, quite
       dreadful.

AJ: But I don't understand, Momma. I mean, what happened?

EZ: I'll tell you what happened. Your father organised a civic
       welcome for him. Everybody was there to greet him. The
       schools had a holiday. The square was packed with invalids
       on stretchers. People had been brought in for miles for him
       to heal them. The amount of work involved was enormous - you
       know how meticulous your father is about these things. He
       couldn't have done more if the Governor General himself had
       been coming. And what happened, you say? Well, this Jesus
       Davidson just ignored us. Deliberately ignored us. There we
       all were on the jetty - he came across the lake by boat, y'see
       - and we were waiting. Your father in his mayoral robes and
       chain, all the council members, the Chief Constable, the Medical
       Officer of Health, the town band - everybody. There was to be
       a civic lunch in the Town Hall and the streets were lined with
       people and children all waiting to see him go by. And afterwards
       he was to walk round the square and heal invalids. But instead -
       instead - oh, Anne, just thinking about it makes me go hot and
       cold all over.

AJ: Momma, please. Don't upset yourself. I'm sure it wasn't as bad
       as you .....

EZ: It was awful, Anne. Really awful. We saw the boat coming and
       Davidson standing in it, shading his eyes with his hand, not
       looking our way at all - staring up at the cemetery on the
       hillside beyond the town - you know, down the coast a bit. And
       suddenly the boat turned away and started sailing in towards the
       beach below the cemetery wall. I couldn't believe it, dear. I
       just couldn't believe my eyes. We all stood there looking stupid,
       dressed up for the occasion and the band all ready to play, and the
       boat sailed away from us and left us standing there.

AJ: But why? I mean, he must've seen you.

EZ: Oh, he saw us all right. That's what was so awful.

AJ: But what did he go to the cemetery for, Momma? I mean .....

EZ: That's what we were wondering. 'What's the man playing at?'

the Town Clerk said. And then we heard it.

AJ: Heard what, Momma?

EZ: That dreadful howling and sobbing noise. Screeching and
        wailling enough to make your blood run cold. We all knew who
        it was , of course. Old Schizo.

AJ: Old .....? Oh, you mean the fisherman who .....

EZ: That's right, dear. You remember. It was - what - oh, a
        couple of years ago now. He was out on the lake with his nets
        when his house caught fire.

AJ: And his wife and two children were trapped in the flames and .....

EZ: Burned to death, poor dears. He hauled his nets and started
        rowing, but of course it was too late to do anything. And it
        turned his brain, poor man.

AJ: He's still up there, is he? In the cemetery among the graves?

EZ: Yes, dear. At least, he was until last Tuesday. Poor Old
        Schizo - I mean, we have tried dear, you know that. Had him in
        hospital twice but he always breaks out and runs riot through
        the town. Very dangerous and violent. It's not his fault, of
        course. Half the time he doesn't know who he is or where he is.
        Your father's agonised over him - we all have. But there's
        nothing anyone can do. In the end we just had to leave him up
        there, muttering and howling among the gravestones like some sort
        of animal. I mean, people take food out and leave it on the wall
        for him. But you can't get near him. He's too violent and you
        can't trust him not to just suddenly fly at you. He's all ragged
        and shaggy and filthy dirty of course. Dreadful.

AJ: Momma, are you saying that Jesus Davidson went to see Old Schizo?

EZ: Yes, dear, he did. Left us all standing on the jetty like
        idiots and got out of his boat and climbed over the cemetery wall
        and walked up the hill to see a madman. Now you know why we felt
        so insulted, so - well, affronted. I mean, all those poor souls
        waiting patiently in the square, lying on their stretchers in the
        sun, hoping he would come and heal them. And your father and I
        and all the Council ready with little speeches of welcome. And a
        couple of children with posies of flowers to give him And he
        turned his back on us and went to see a crazy man who's been
        nothing but trouble and a source of embarrassment to us for years.

AJ: Yes, I see. Very awkward.

EZ: Is that all you can say? **Very awkward.**

AJ: No, sorry, Momma. Of course it was dreadful for you. I
        can see that. So what did you do?

EZ: We went after him, I'm afraid dear.

AJ: To the cemetery? You all went up to the cemetery to .....?

EZ: It was a case of having to, Anne. Don't think I wanted to
        go up there because I most certainly didn't. But all the
        people started running along the beach and your father said
        we should follow them. I didn't think it was a good idea
        and said so, but he was quite determined. 'My place is with
        the people,' he said, 'if they go, I must go too.' I said,
        'Matthew, be reasonable. I can't go traipsing along the beach
        in these shoes.' I'd bought a new outfit, you see dear,
        specially for the occasion - blue silk dress and a **big** picture
        hat and high heeled shoes.

AJ: Oh, Momma, poor you. I feel sorry for .....

EZ: Thank you dear. Anyway, your father agreed - and just went off
        and left me there on the jetty with all those bandsmen gawping
        at me.

AJ: What on earth did you do, Momma?

EZ: I took the car. Told the driver to take me along the top road
        and drop me at the cemetery gates. It's not more than five
        minutes's drive, of course, but it seemed like hours. I was
        all trembly and - y'know, choked-up. I kept thinking of that
        dreadful lunatic thrashing about up there and wondering if
        he'd attack your father and then run amok through all the
        people and .....

AJ: Oh, Momma, how awful for you. I can just imagine how you
        must've .....

EZ: Yes, dear. Actually, it was all rather an anti-climax. When
        I got out of the car and went into the cemetery, there was Jesus
        Davidson and Old Schizo with him, sitting on a gravestone, the
        two of them talking quietly together, smiling and chatting as
        though nothing had happened. Your father was there, too. And

the Town Clerk and all the rest, standing in a bunch a few yards away, looking a bit put out. Your father was rather pale, all that running along the beach hadn't done him any good - but otherwise all right. He beckoned me over and put his arm round me and said there was nothing to worry about.

AJ: And what did Jesus Davidson do then, Momma?

EZ: Do? Nothing dear. Just went on chatting to Old Schizo as though nobody else was there. It was most upsetting. It really was. I mean, I know he's only a working-class man, no background, no breeding. But your father and I - and everybody else - we were all in our best clothes - obviously important people - and he just - well, ignored us.

AJ: I expect he was making sure Old Schizo was really .....

EZ: That's right, dear. Make excuses for the man. Everybody else does.

AJ: No, Momma I'm not. Only, well, I can see how important it must've been for him to - well, concentrate on his patient.

EZ: Oh, I'm sure. Very important.

AJ: Don't be bitter, Momma, please. What happened then?

EZ: What? Oh, nothing much. Nothing of any interest.

AJ: Momma don't be like that. I really want to know.

EZ: Well, the Town Clerk cleared his throat then, rather loudly and Davidson looked up and said, 'Ah, there you all are.' As if we'd been invisible until then. 'Look', he said, 'my friend here needs some decent clothes.' Which was true enough. Old Schizo was in rags - no shirt, no socks, just an old, torn jacket and a pair of ragged trousers. Awful.

AJ: But you say he was quite calm?

EZ: Oh, quite calm. Rather smug as a matter of fact. Davidson said, 'You all look very prosperous and important. I'm sure between you, you can fix him up with a few things, can't you? He's quite himself again, y'know. Quite cured and normal. I think the least you can do is welcome him back.' Honestly Anne, it was so embarrassing; expecting us to give the man our .....

I mean, your father is the Mayor, after all. He can't
be expected to take his official coat off and give it to -
well, just anybody.

AJ: I suppose not, Momma. Only .....

EZ: Only what? I mean, we only had Davidson's word the man was
cured. Oh, he looked normal enough, I'll admit that. But
permanently cured? I doubted it. So did the Health Officer.
He saw the Town Clerk start to unbutton his coat and said,
'Forget it, John. Give him your coat and he'll have it in
shreds before you know it.'

AJ: And did he? Give him his coat, I mean.

EZ: No he didn't, Anne. And quite right too. Your father was
all for asking Jesus to come back to the square but the Chief
Constable ruled that out. I must say I was relieved. If
Davidson chose to insult us all by deliberately boycotting our
reception committee to go chasing after a raving lunatic, I
didn't see we were under any obligation to invite him back for
a civic lunch.

AJ: But what about all the people waiting to be cured, Momma.

EZ: That's what your father said. Too soft-hearted by half. I
told him so too. Enough, after all, is enough, I said. We've
all been treated like .....

AJ: So he didn't go back with you?

EZ: What? No. No, he didn't. In any case, the crowd didn't want
him by that time. Seeing Old Schizo sitting there so calmly
seemed to bother them some how. You know how superstitious
some of these lakeside people are. They think insanity is
caused by the devil, so only a devil can cure it. Anyway there
was a lot of muttering and grumbling and soon it became obvious
even to your father that inviting Davidson back to town was not
a good idea. So in the end we just left him there in the cemetery
with Old Schizo.

AJ: Oh, Momma, you didn't

EZ: We certainly did, dear. Of course it was a terrible let-down
after all the trouble we'd gone to - the civic reception and the
lunch and everything

AJ: Yes

EZ: Seeing the invalids leave for home was **the** worst part.
Poor dears, they looked so desolate, so - well, betrayed.
I think it is wicked to raise people's hopes the way that
man does and then just pass them by and do nothing to help
them.

AJ: But, Momma, it was hardly his fault. If you didn't ask him
back, how could he .....?

EZ: Don't split **hairs**, Anne. Of course it was his fault. If
he'd behaved properly, come to the jetty the way he should've
done, met your father and I and been taken to the Town Hall,
he could've spent the whole afternoon healing people.

AJ: Well, at least he healed Old Schizo, Momma.

EZ: That's as maybe, dear. I mean, we don't know. Not for sure.
Some say he went off in the boat afterwards with Davidson and
the others. If so, I wish joy to him. Sooner or later he'll
turn nasty again and then they'll realise what we've had to put
up with all this time.

AJ: How has Daddy taken it all?

EZ: Badly, **dear**. He's very upset about it. He seems depressed -
y'know, withdrawn - and that's not like him. I get the feeling
he thinks we've somehow made a mistake. There's a rather
unpleasant bit of gossip going round the district - all the local
villages. They're calling us the town that turned God away. Isn't
that awful. And so unfair. God, indeed. What blasphemous
nonsense. He was just a carpenter's son who got his priorities
wrong.

AJ: Oh, Momma I don't know. Are you quite sure he .....?

EZ: Oh, Anne, for goodness sake, child. You're as bad as your
father. Of course I'm sure. You've never met Davidson, have
you?

AJ: Not actually met him, no. But .....

15/8

EZ: There you are then. I have, I'm sorry to say. And you can
        take it from me, dear, he's not at all the sort of person one
        could introduce to one's friends.

        END OF EXERPT

        COPIES TO:

                His Grace the High Priest
                The Metropolitan Commissioner
                Head of Security, Imperial Army HQ, Jerusalem
                Divisional Commander, Special Division

Typical. The man has no sense of occasion.

THOMSON'S KOSHER BUTCHER

3 High Street,
Lydda.
Tel: Lydda 351

The Headmaster,
Rabbi Sanballet School,
Jaffa.

Dear Sir,

    Thank you for your letter offering me an appointment next
Tuesday, which I gladly accept and will arrive promptly with my
son, Ezra. I note that you have other parents to see that day so
I am taking the liberty of writing about my son now so that you
will have a clearer idea of his character when we meet and it will
save time on the day. As you will see from the Enrolment Form I
sent previously his education has so far been rather sketchy, indeed
he has scarcely been in school for a complete week since he began
at the age of six - until this last year, that is. The reason for
this is quite simply his health. He was until a year ago an
epileptic, suffering two and sometimes as many as five fits every
twenty-four hours for weeks at a time. That he has progressed so
far as he has (he is literate and numerate and has some knowledge
of elementary history, geography and basic science) is due very
largely to the devoted care and patience of my wife who has struggled
to fill the enormous gaps in his school attendance record by teaching
him at home until a year ago, since when he has made quite remarkable
strides according to his teachers. But he is, of course, barely able
to meet the required standard specified in your prospectus, although
his IQ test shows him to be an intelligent boy, quick to learn.

    The important thing is, he is no longer an epileptic. All
traces of the disease have vanished. For more than a year now he has
been free from fits. If you are very sceptical about this (and I
imagine you will be) perhaps I may venture some explanation? I will
not bore you with too many details of what it is like to bring up a
chronic epileptic. Suffice it to say that as his eleventh birthday
approached my wife and I, reviewing a long and daunting history of
fits and physical damage (on a number of occasions he fell into the
fire, twice he was rescued from drowning having fallen into the
river in a fit), could only pray that we would outlive our son, that
he would not be left alone in the world with years of life in front

of him and nobody to look after him. And then the miracle happened.

We were visiting friends and Ezra of course was with us. It was in fact one of his better days since he managed to get through most of the morning without trouble. But just before lunch he had a major fit, which was quite frightening to witness. When it was over, our friends mentioned Jesus Davidson. We had heard of him, of course, although I myself was very dubious about his powers and in any case we have had our hopes dashed on too many occasions over the years to put any kind of faith in doctors, much less faith healers. However, our friends insisted they had personal knowledge of people who had been cured by Davidson and in the end though with reluctance, I agreed to take the boy to him. As luck would have it, Davidson was expected in the village that afternoon. When Ezra and I got to the square some of his followers were there waiting for him with a big crowd already gathered round them. I asked if they could arrange for Ezra to see Davidson and one of them said, 'We can do better than that. Bring the lad here and we'll heal him for you.' I wasn't very keen about this because they didn't look much like healers to me, rather coarsely-spoken and on the rough side. However, they tried, without success. All that happened was that Ezra had a fit, brought on no doubt by the excitement and the noise of the crowd gaping and pointing at him though he were some freak out of a circus. The followers of Davidson continued their antics, shouting their prayers in a most vulgar fashion and struggling to keep their hands on Ezra's head as he writhed and shook in the fit. I'm afraid I got very angry, pulled them away and picked the boy up in my arms. The fit was passing and he settled into an uneasy doze.

I decided enough was enough and was just about to push my way out of the crowd and take him home when Davidson arrived, looking tired and strained. 'What's going on here?' he said, rather impatiently I thought. One of his men explained. 'We tried, Master,' they said. 'We really tried.' He nodded, watching me. I said, 'Not very successfully, as you can see,' and he said almost off-handedly, 'The gift is not for everyone, my friend. It demands great concentration and prayer.' Which sounded to me like a cast-iron alibi. It's never the healers who fail, always the poor victims who don't have enough faith. Then he said, 'What's the matter with the boy?' So I told him and didn't mince my words, either. He listened quietly, nodding now and then and when I'd finished he said, 'So what d'you want me to do?' It seemed a peculiar question with Ezra there, white and limp after the fit. I was on the brink of turning away in disgust when something made me say, 'Heal him, please. I want you to heal him if you can.'

I saw a little flash of anger in his eyes. 'If I can?' he said.
'If I can? Oh no,my friend it's not if I can. It's if you believe
I can. Do you?' And again I was tempted just to turn on my heels and
walk away, what with all those people watching, quiet now, tensed up,
waiting. But again something stopped me. I saw his eyes change their
expression, not angry now, more compassionate, as if he were willing
me to believe. I thought, well what have we got to lose? Easy enough
to say I believe. So I nodded. 'Yes, I believe,' I said and his eyes
bored into me, hard, sharp. He knew I was lying, knew I didn't
believe. And I said, this time with complete honesty, 'I believe.
Help me to believe more. Please help me to believe enough.' And then
he smiled, a tired, relieved sort of smile and told me to let Ezra
stand up. I put the boy on his feet and Davidson touched his head
with one hand 'Well, son,' he said. 'How d'you feel now?' And Ezra
looked at him and said, 'I feel — I feel very well, thank you, sir.'
And I saw his face and all the pain had gone out of it and his eyes
were bright and calm and he grinned at me like the schoolboy he is.
'I'm fine, Dad,' he said. 'Honest. I'm all right again.'

And so it has proved. We took him home that day, watching him
like a hawk, waiting for that first fit to start, but it didn't, not
that day, not that night, not at all since Jesus Davidson touched him,
and that's just over a year ago. He's eating well, sleeping peacefully
through the night, full of energy and life and happiness. All he needs
now to set him up is a good education and the chance to develop his
talents. If you can find a place for him in the school I can promise
you it won't be wasted. I don't of course know what your opinion of
Jesus Davidson is. I understand the authorities in Jerusalem are
seeking to discredit him, calling him a charlatan. Apparently his
theological views are suspect and of course I can't speak about that.
I can only say that he has given us our son back a normal, healthy
child.

May I say to you, sir, what I said in a different context to
Jesus Davidson? Please, if you can, help our son.

Yours faithfully,

Peter Thomson

Peter Thomson

LETTER FROM J SANBALLET, TO JESUS BARABBUS.
INTERCEPTED 12 DECEMBER '80 AND TRANSCRIBED
DUE TO ILLEGIBILITY OF HANDWRITING.

Safe House 4

Barabbus old son,

Give the bearer of this a big welcome will you, mate,
because as well as this letter he's bringing you a little
present, see? Like twelve thousand quid in used notes.
That's right, twelve thou. What the guy who's come up with
it calls a modest contribution to our fighting fund.

Like I was in the back room behind Joe's store up in
Nablus, checking through his log book (Roman troop movements
on the main Jerusalem/Damascus road) when he bobs through
the door from the shop and says there's somebody wants to
see me. Which shook me a bit because nobody was supposed
to know I was in town. So I asked Joe how this guy knew
I was there and he said he'd told him. 'Now why in the
world did you go and do that, Joe?' I said - or words to
that effect, and Joe said he hadn't mentioned my name
(which was big of him) but the guy had said he wanted to
get in touch with - well, one of us, like. And Joe had
sort of taken it from there.

Anyway, the damage was done then, so I decided I'd
better have a quick shufti at this character and keep my
options open, so I dodged through into the shop. I had
him sized, measured and classified as soon as I set eyes
on him. A toff, mate, that's what he was. Hundred
guinea suit, silk shirt, money running out of both ears.
Gentry with a capital G, estates in Galilee, villa in
Haifa, town house in Jerusalem, a yacht or two - nothing
flash.

'Good afternoon to you,' he said, polite like.
Educated accent, bit of a Roman drawl. You know the

kind. Blue-blooded Jew with one foot in the synagogue
and the other in Pilate's front room. I had a quick shufti
through the shop window and sure enough there was this
socking great car outside, white convertible that had cost
more to buy than the average block of flats and needed a
small fortune just to keep it on the road. Well, I mean,
you don't toddle round in one of those if all you've got
behind you is a two-acre small holding and a couple of
lousy Premium Bonds.

I asked what I could do for him and he grinned.
'It's what I can do for you, friend,' he said. 'That's if
you're who I think you are.' So I spun him my usual cover
story about being a rep with a big wholesale grocers up
in Damascus travelling the towns and villages trying to
make an honest penny. 'I don't think so,' he said. 'I
think you're in the PLA.' Of course I denied it. 'People's
Liberation Army, sir?' I said all innocent. 'Me? No way.'

He shrugged. 'Pity,' he said. 'I've got a bit of
spare cash. Thought I'd make a modest contribution to the
fighting fund.' And then I saw this suitcase on the floor
beside him. 'How much?' I said. He grinned again.
'Twelve thou, actually.'

So I told Joe to pull the blinds down and lock the
door and took His Nibs into the back room and sat him
down. 'OK, Buster,' I said. 'What's the story?'

Barabbus old son, you aren't going to believe this.
I was dead right about this guy, rich young aristo with
all the trimmings. Parents dead, unmarried, title and
fortune all his. But he wasn't very chuffed about it,
see? So he trots off to see the rabbi, but the rabbi's

no help, well they never are, are they? So he's back to
square one and moody as all get-out. Then he meets up
with this Jesus Davidson from Nazareth. And you know what
I think about him. I mean, he says all the right things
about freedom and justice for the poor and all that, same
as we do. But what does he do about it? Nothing. OK,
I know, he's got religion and that always pulls a man down
in the end. Anyway, this rich guy asks his advice. How
to make life worth living sort of thing, put a bit of zip
back in it. And you know what Davidson said? Sell up and
give the bread away to feed the poor. Which is fair enough.

But this millionaire lad doesn't think so. Not at
the time, anyway. But when he'd thought about it a bit
he decided to take Davidson's advice, so he sold up and
cashed in. Made a few hefty donations to worthy causes
like hospitals and orphanages and Help the Aged — that
sort of thing. Which left him with a bit over — like
twelve thousand nicker — for us. When he opened that
suitcase and showed me the lolly I nearly had a heart
attack. I mean, think what we can buy with it. No more
knocking off Roman small-arms, we can nip up to Libya and
buy our own. 'You won't regret this,' I said.

He nodded, like he was not too sure, and began to
talk a bit more. Said he was looking for something to
make sense out of life and he reckoned getting rid of
the bread was a start, but only a start. Like, there was
still something missing and he didn't know what it was.
'Jesus Davidson's got the answer,' he said. 'He's poor
and he's got no home to call his own and half the police
in Israel are gunning for him. But he's happy, really
happy. Fulfilled, if you see what I mean?'

I didn't, but I had the sense not to say so. 'Once

we get shot of our Latin-speaking friends things'll be
better,' I said.

        'I hope so,' he said, but he didn't sound very
convinced. He smiled a bit sketchily. 'I don't suppose
I'm making much sense to you.' Which was typical of his
sort. They always seem to think our kind are pig-ignorant
just because we've jacked everything in and gone under-
ground to ditch the Romans. I felt like telling him about
some of the lads we've got working for us - educated
characters, professional men. I mean, we're not all
illiterate louts. But I didn't bother. That's our image
I suppose and no amount of talking's going to change it.
Instead I said, 'I see you've still got your motor.' He
shook his head. 'Only for an hour. It's been sold and
I'm on my way to deliver it now.'

        Poor little devil, I felt sorry for him then. He'd
done all he could, made the big gesture and beggared himself and he still wasn't happy. Maybe he was still in
shock, of course. Ladling out that kind of lolly must do
something to your system. Or maybe he was just soft-
centred like Davidson. Enough guts to take the first step
on the road to freedom, but not enough to follow through.
Still, that's his bad luck, and our good luck. With this
twelve thou, if we play our cards right, I reckon that
little show you've got planned for next Passover might
just come off. Up the revolution, eh.

                L'hayim,

                Jake

I have no sympathy with these ruffians but am
relieved to have this evidence of their rejection
of Davidson. Allied to them he could be
extremely dangerous.

                        6.

Casual Ward
Municipal Hostel
Jericho

20.3.81

Jesus Davidson
c/o Martha and Mary Magdalene
Corner Cottage
Bethany

Dear Sir,

I wonder if you remember me, Sir, Bartimaeus of Jericho.
The blind beggar whose sight you restored a couple of months
ago.

I hope you will forgive me for writing to you. You've
done so much for me it seems churlish to ask for more help.
Almost ungrateful. And I'm not that, Sir, believe me I'm not.
I'll always be grateful to you for giving me my sight and
changing my life. Only - well, that's the trouble, you see.
My life has changed and I can't cope with it.

I've been a professional beggar for nearly forty years.
When my parents died my elder brother and his wife very kindly
took me in. My sister-in-law is a good organiser. It was she
who found me that pitch in the main street, right opposite the
bank. She led me to it every morning and came to take me back
home again in the evening. The money I collected I paid over
to her. In return they fed and clothed me and gave me a place
to sleep in their house. And that was my life for forty years.
And now, Sir, it's all changed. I can't beg anymore because
everyone knows I'm no longer blind. So I don't earn anything.
And my brother and his wife have made it clear to me that they
can't afford to keep me without payment. Which is understandable,
of course.

I've tried to get a job, naturally. But nobody here wants
to know. I've no special skill or trade, you see, and whilst
I'm willing to learn nobody thinks it's economic to spend
money training a man already in his fifties with only a few working

years in front of him. I've tried to get labouring jobs -
gardening mainly. But, of course, although I can see the
plants and weeds, I can't tell which is which. Being able
to see is one thing - and a marvellous thing, too, Sir,
don't misunderstand me - but being able to understand what
you see - that's something else again. Everything looks so
strange and different - not at all the way it used to feel
when I was blind and had to use my hands to discover things.
I really need about a year just to get used to recognising
objects and getting to know what they are and how they work.
And that takes money, and I have no money.

There's another problem too. And that - if you'll
forgive me, Sir - is you. I'm afraid you're not very popular
here in Jericho. My brother and his wife don't like you
because you've taken away one of the main sources of their
income. And most of the important people in the town haven't
forgiven you for Zacchaeus.

You remember Zacchaeus? The tax collector you stayed with
when you were here that time? The man everybody hated because
they knew he was cheating them and anyway he was working for
Rome? When you accepted his invitation to stay at his house
it caused a lot of offence, I'm afraid. Some of the town's
VIP's were very keen to have you as their guest, you see.
And when you chose to go home with Zacchaeus they were bitterly
offended. People are like that, aren't they? I expect you've
found that out for yourself.

Anyway, they've sort of lumped Zacchaeus and I together
in their minds, you see. And that doesn't help much. I
went to see the Mayor a couple of days ago. They were adver-
tising a job in the parks department - well, it was cleaning
the public lavatories, in fact. Not much of a job, but one
I felt I could probably manage fairly well. But the Mayor
was not prepared to offer me the job. 'You can't expect any
favours from me, Bartimaeus,' he said. 'Not with the sort
of company you keep. Why don't you ask your friend Jesus,
eh? He's interested in beggars and collaborators. I'm not.'

Well, Sir, I'm desperate enough now to take his advice and write
to you. My brother has told me I've got to get out of his house
by the end of next week - partly because he can't afford to keep
me and partly because having me here isn't doing his business any
good. Nobody else in the town wants to know me, much less put me
up rent free. I've tried to find Zacchaeus but he's moved away.
Was more or less driven out, in fact. And if anybody knows where
he's living now, they aren't saying. So it's you or nobody, Sir.
You've given me my sight and a new lease of life. Can you help
me now to use it?

      If you can't, I'll have to move to another town, wear dark
glasses and pretend to be blind again. That way I can make a
living of sorts. But I don't want to do that. It would be a
terrible waste of your gift to me.

      As I say, Sir, it's not that I'm ungrateful. Please don't
think that. I wake up every morning and see the sky and the
sunlight and the mountains above the town and I thank God for
you. But I'm not really a fit person to handle a gift of this
kind without a great deal of help., I'm like a baby, really,
you see. As though I'd been born aged fifty-four.

      The public letter-writer I'm dictating this to (I still
haven't learned to read and write, I'm afraid) has just told me
there's a rumour you've been arrested. He says on a charge of
treason. I hope it's not true, Sir. If anything should happen
to you I'd really be on my own.

                          Yours sincerely,

                          Bartimaeus, His Mark

One more example of the damage Davidson
    has done to ordinary people.

  18.4.81

PROCURATOR OF JUDEA AND SAMARIA
THE RESIDENCY
JERUSALEM

PHOTOCOPIED
22 APR 81
DATE _____
SIGNED *al Habbuk*

FROM: Pontius Pilate, Governor of Judea

TO: Cassius Sempronus, Senator

MONDAY

    Cass, I'm sending this in the Diplomatic Bag under my special seal,
top secret. It's Monday morning and the bag won't go out till this time
next week. By then the crisis - if it is a crisis - will be on the Senate
Order Paper for debate. So I'd like you to have my own off-the-record,
on-the-spot thinking - what happens, as it happens. Because if this
thing does run a temperature I just could be looking for a good lawyer by
the end of the month. And I don't know a better one than you.

    OK. Crises are a built-in hazard for any Provincial Governor -
especially if his Province is Judea. I budgeted for that when I accepted
the appointment. Jews and trouble go together like midge bites and itching.
But there are crises and crises. And this one looks like being the grand-
daddy of them all. If it breaks. And I think it will.

    The source of the infection is a man called Jesus. A jobbing carpenter
from Nazareth, which is a flyblown little wog town up in the north of the
Province. He's one of these self-educated chaps with the gift of the gab.
You know the sort; a lot of mouth and just a touch of magic. A real
crowd puller. And religious, of course.

    This place is lousy with religion. Which isn't my special subject, I'm
afraid. I've never been able to see the point of it, to be quite honest.
Fair dealing, just laws, a stable economy and the muscle to hold it all
together - in my opinion that's all we need. The good old Pax Romana in
fact. But these Jews are into religion in spades. Drag God into everything
from interest rates on a loan to what to have for dinner and how to cook it.
The way they've got it figured, the Church runs the State and I'm only in
the Residency by courtesy of the High Priest.

    That's Caiaphas. A very unpleasant gentleman indeed. Smooth, clever,
vindictive as a discarded mistress. And a born poker player. He runs this
Province. Secret Police, paid informers, his own private army - the lot.

He's got it set up like a jigsaw puzzle; every piece interlocking and himself in the middle. All I'm expected to do is show the flag on state
occasions and stand by to rescue him if the peasants get stroppy. That way
he keeps his own image benevolent and projects us as the muscle-men who
move in with pick-axe handles when life gets a bit fraught.

Like it almost did yesterday afternoon.

This Jesus character staged a bit of a demo in the Temple courtyard.
Rode into the city with his gang - and they're a pretty moronic bunch
according to Caiaphas. Country oiks, most of 'em. One brain between
twelve and not a very big brain at that. Anyway, they put up quite a
show and the whole place went into a sort of politico-religious ferment.
Hail to the King and God bless Israel. That sort of stuff. Harmless
enough, I suppose. I mean, it's going to take a lot more than twelve
thick heavyweights to inconvenience my chaps in the Tenth Legion. But
the city's filling up with pilgrims for the Passover and they seemed to
think it was something special. Fulfilment of a prophecy or some such
rubbish. Things looked a bit ugly for a while and I thought we were in
for some fairly solid aggro. Perhaps it would have been better that way.
At least, at that stage, we could have contained it.

He made his play in the outer court of the Temple. I'll say this
for him, Cass, he knows how to pick his location. And his timing's
near perfect. The outer court is a sort of cross between a cattle market
and a fun fair. They've got this sacrificial system, you see. They buy
lambs and bullocks and pigeons in the courtyard and hand them over to the
butcher-priests for slaughter and burning. Messy business. Blood and
guts all over the place. Millions of flies, of course, and the smell is
appalling. It's an extraordinary mentality which envisages God as being
someone who sits up in heaven enjoying the stench of melting animal fat.

But the real trouble-centre is the money-changing system. The trick
is, the priests won't accept Roman currency in payment for sacrificial
animals. So the peasants have to change it for the special Temple money
- which is valueless outside the Temple precincts. Of course, there's a
rake-off. Two, in fact. One for the priests and another, much bigger,
for the money-changers. You can imagine how that rankles. If anybody
really wants to start a riot, that's the place to do it.

And that's exactly what Jesus did yesterday afternoon. Made a bit of
a speech, got the crowd nicely-worked up and then - timing it beautifully
- deliberately went through the courtyard kicking over the stalls of the
money-changers. Ably assisted, I may say, by every poor little bastard
of a tenant farmer who objected to paying through the nose for a couple
of lice-ridden pigeons or a quarter share in an under-nourished, maggot-
infested lamb. It was, I gather, quite a party.

Colonel Macer - old Iron Guts Macer of the Tenth - brought his chaps
to red alert status and it looked like we were on our merry way. But in

the event it just faded. One minute Jesus was there, whipping them up to
a frenzy, all righteous indignation and freedom for the masses. The next
- he'd quit. Shut up, backed-off and split. End of story.

Or is it? Caiaphas doesn't think so. He keeps floating in here oozing
doom and disaster. Perhaps he's right to be worried. Perhaps it's not all
over yet. Perhaps it's just beginning.

But beginning what? I've read the file on this Jesus character and
he's strictly junior league, Cass. No muscle. No organisation. Nothing
but a silver tongue and a line of slightly romantic idealism that women
especially seem to find irresistible. So why am I uptight about him? I
don't know. But I am. I don't know how or when, but I think we're on a
collision course with something pretty nasty.

Ah well, the next few days will see it develop. Or not. I'll leave
this now and add to it as things progress. If they do. I'm probably just
wasting your time, Cass. I hope so. But I've got this pricking in my
thumbs that tells me I'm not.

THURSDAY

Hello again. Thursday now and we're still in business. I keep telling
myself the whole thing was a false alarm. I just wish I could believe it.

I've taken all the usual precautions, naturally. The way I **always** do
when we're coming up to the Passover weekend. All leave cancelled. Street
patrols doubled. The entire garrison on twenty-four hours readiness. So
far it's been a total waste of time and I can imagine what the troops are
saying about me. Still, you can't always be popular, can you?

This Passover thing's a bit of a headache at the best of times. It's
a religious festival (what else, in this God-haunted country?) but it's
got a lot of political charisma. Basically it celebrates the Jewish
Freedom March out of Egypt way back when. They've wrapped it up in the
usual mumbo-jumbo about God and the Promised Land. But what they're really
saying, in a cautious sort of way, is: Rome out, our own King in. Which
isn't on, of course. They get away with it by pretending their King (when
he comes) will be a sort of God-figure coming down to reign in peace. But
I've seen the reports of our up-country patrols and they don't make
reassuring reading. The hills are lousy with guerrilla troops just waiting
for somebody to pass the word. So it's not all pie-in-the-sky stuff.

Up to now there hasn't actually been a King candidate at the Passover.
They do their celebrating on a sort of this-time-next-year-maybe basis.
But this year they've got a candidate all right. Jesus Davidson.

I've had a couple of long sessions with Caiaphas and he seems to be
taking it all very seriously. He doesn't himself think Jesus is the right
man and he's got himself a touch uptight in case the boys in the hills
jump the gun and make a fight of it. My impression is that he's all for

getting rid of us but doesn't fancy the sort of clobbering we'd hand out if the attempt aborted. He doesn't actually say so, of course. He talks to me like a Dutch uncle about public safety and the responsibility of office and all that clap-trap. But I'm getting to know how his mind works and I can see he's pretty shaken underneath.

As you'll appreciate, it makes my position very delicate. Because if this thing does come to the boil - as he seems to think it might - it's going to be yours truly who'll be left holding the baby. And that, my good lawyer friend, is where you'll come in. I hope.

Quite honestly, I don't really see it happening. I've checked out the reports of our agents planted in the crowds when Jesus has been banging the big drum and I must say it all sounds quite innocuous. Some of his ideas aren't at all bad, as a matter-of-fact. A bit far-fetched and idealistic - as you'd expect - but no way can they be called treasonable. Quite the reverse, in fact. He seems to be all for the status quo as far as Rome goes. Pay your taxes. Do what the soldiers tell you. Admirable advice.

No, it's the hierarchy of the Jewish Church he's got his knife into. Knows his stuff too. Some of the things he's been saying are spot-on: about corruption and hypocrisy and one law for the priests and another for the people - that sort of thing. Down with the rich and God bless the poor. It doesn't exactly endear him to Caiaphas, though. And without Caiaphas's support I don't reckon I'd last much more than a month or two. I don't flatter myself that I understand these people. But he does. And I have to rely on his judgement. So if it comes to the crunch I'll have to play it his way.

I don't know, Cass. Religion's all right in church, if you're into that sort of thing. But let loose on the streets - well, that's something else again. A recipe for disaster. If there really is a God, who of us can stand having him breathing down our necks when we're trying to get on with real life?

Ah well, tomorrow's the big day. When the Passover starts. If we get through that we'll be home and dry. I'll let you know.

SATURDAY

Cass, it's all over. I shan't be needing your professional services after all.

Jesus Davidson, self-styled King of the Jews, is dead and buried. His followers are in hiding. Already, tonight, as the city turns out to celebrate after the Passover services, he is virtually forgotten by the crowds.

Caiaphas's secret police picked him up late on Thursday evening. It seems one of his own men turned informer and shopped him. He was hauled

up in front of a special sitting on the Sanhedrin Court and convicted.
The charge, at that stage, was blasphemy. Which carries the death penalty
in Jewish law, but not of course in ours. So by the time they wheeled him
in front of me early yesterday morning they'd changed it to treason.
Which didn't leave me much option but to sign the death warrant. The
Tenth Legion laid on an execution squad, with their usual efficiency and
that was that. We did it in public, I'm afraid. Had to, of course. I
don't like it but when somebody **pops** up and claims he's the true King,
above the law, above Caesar himself - well, you've got to make an example
of him. Or else.

He was in his grave before sunset yesterday evening - which is when the
Passover officially started. Reports this morning from the street patrols
confirm that the situation in the city is normal. The King is dead, long
life the Emperor - at least until this time next year.

So why am I wasting your time with all this? I honestly don't know,
Cass. Except I have to talk to somebody. You see, the whole thing was
processed correctly through the normal legal channels. It was a bit quick,
of course. Had to be, with the Passover looming over us all. But it was
legal. Jesus Davidson was duly tried and found guilty. The fact that, in
my opinion, he was innocent is probably neither here nor there.

He did in fact say he was a King. I wouldn't have signed the warrant
otherwise. I mean, between you and me, Cass, it was a put-up job.
Caiaphas wanted him out of the way because he was a threat to the Jewish
Establishment. But the man was no more a traitor to Rome than I am.
'My Kingdom is not of this world,' he said to me. And I believed him.
But Caiaphas had us both in a corner. Early in the morning as it was,
by the time I'd finished questioning Jesus, the old fox had whipped up
a mob from somewhere and had them howling for blood. If I had refused
to play his game he would have organised a mass riot. And (more
important) sent a report to Rome over my head about the Governor's
support for a convicted traitor. So my hands were tied, damn him.

'You've done a wise thing, Your Excellency,' he said to me late
yesterday afternoon. 'For the first time in three years this country
is at peace with itself.' I suppose he's right, but I don't like it. I
said as much to him and he smiled, that snide, poker-player's smile of
his, and said smoothly, 'Better one man should die than the whole nation
be imperilled.' Which is true enough. Only - only the way he said it
- so rehearsed, so smug - I knew he was lying. Whatever else he was,
Jesus was no blood-thirsty Nationalist. He was a healer, not a destroyer.
A man of peace. I know because I talked to him.

I know what you'll say, Cass - if I ever bother now to send you this.
'These things happen. The innocent suffer. Justice, in the end, is a
hit-and-miss affair.' All the comforting bromides. And you're probably
right at that. Here we are in the middle of the Passover and not a
suspicion of trouble. Everything easy and normal. Everybody happy. One
man's death is a small price to pay for that, I suppose.

And yet - it should never have happened. Caiaphas has tricked me and I don't like it. I don't like it at all. Being out-smarted by the greasy little ..... Oh, to hell with it, Cass, that's not what's bugging me. It's Jesus Davidson, not Caiaphas. He's the one I can't get out of my mind.

He was sorry for me - you know that? Absurd, isn't it? Standing there yesterday morning after one hell of a night - tried, convicted, flogged, abused by the troops (you know what they did, Cass? Dressed the poor devil up in a purple robe and shoved a crown of thorns on his head and pretended to pay homage to him as a King. Bastards.) - anyway, there he was in front of me bloodied and tired, just about out on his feet. And he was sorry for me. For me. As if he knew I was helpless to save him. 'Look,' I said to him, 'I'm the Governor, right? I'm the law here. I've only got to raise my hand and you're a dead man.' And d'you know, Cass, he smiled. Actually smiled. He said, 'You have no power over me. I have only to ask my Father and he will immediately send an army of angels to rescue me.' Pathetic, of course. His mind was obviously beginning to go. Not surprising after what they'd done to him. But there was something about him - something in his voice, in his eyes - that frightened me. If you condemn a villain to death and he curses you - well, fair enough. That's his privilege. But if you sign away the life of an innocent man and he - well, forgives you. Looks at you not with hatred but with compassion .....

Odd, isn't it? You work up a sweat about losing control of the Province, take what measures you legally can to safeguard your position and hope like hell it'll sort itself out. And when it does, all you've got is a nasty taste in your mouth and the feeling that somehow you've betrayed yourself.

SUNDAY

Cass, there's something very strange going on here. It's Sunday night now, the Passover's finished, everything's back to normal. On the surface, that is. Underneath, it's a different story.

The thing is, the word is out that Jesus Davidson - the man we topped for treason last Friday - is back in circulation.

I know it's crazy. I know that. Anywhere else it would just be dismissed as a bit of wild superstition. But not here. This is Jerusalem, remember. In this town God is still reckoned with and superstition's the name of the game. If enough people say Jesus is alive again the fact that it's impossible won't make the slightest difference. It's just the sort of miraculous nonsense those hard men holed-up in the hills need to get them started. And if that happens, we're in trouble. Big trouble.

Caiaphas has been here most of the afternoon. Very controlled and dead-pan - the way he always is. But he's a worried man for all that. I could almost hear his brain clicking. He says the rumour is absurd, of course. The way he sees it, somebody's snatched the body and hidden it. A straight-forward bit of grave-robbing, in fact. That's the line he's taking, anyway. And of course it makes sense. I said as much to him. 'Find the body and we're home and dry,' I said. 'Shouldn't be too difficult.'

He agreed, but without much enthusiasm. And that's not like him. Usually there's nothing he enjoys more than to let those secret police thugs of his loose on the city. Like most religious fanatics, he's into terror tactics in a big way. So I'm wondering why this time he's a bit hesitant. Unless, of course, he doesn't believe his own theory. And that's odd too, because he had the grave guarded, you see. Almost as if he expected some-thing like this to happen. I did quiz him about that, actually, and he was evasive and embarrassed. Natural enough, I suppose. He's very touchy about his little private army and if the grave was robbed it doesn't do much for their image, does it? Which only confirms my suspicions. I mean, he must be really twitched if he's prepared to sacrifice the honour of his crack troops to cover up the truth.

But what is the truth? If the grave was not robbed, what's the alternative? It's empty, that's for sure. So where is Jesus Davidson? Alive again?

He thought he was God, Cass. D'you know that? The son of a small-town north country joiner and he thought he was God. Caiaphas admitted as much to me this afternoon. Said that was why he had to get rid of Jesus. Why I was brought in at the last minute to sign the death warrant. It WAS blasphemy, you see, not treason. Now he tells me.

God, what a mess. And so damned unfair. I tried, y'know Cass. To save him. I really did try. Friday morning, when I was through questioning him and knew he was innocent, I went out on to the balcony and offered to release him as the Passover Prisoner. It's one of the local traditions. A sort of religious amnesty. But those bastards down there in the street, they didn't want to know. 'Give us Barabbas,' they shouted back. Now he is a villain. A real, 22 carat heavy man. Terrorist. Saboteur. Political agitator. A walking menace if ever I saw one. And I turned him loose, Cass. Five years we've been after him and lost God knows how many men trying to catch him. And when, in the end, we get lucky and grab him, what happens? I let him go. Gave him his freedom and chopped Jesus Davidson.

Caiaphas says he was mad. Jesus, I mean. But he didn't seem mad to me. Unless an overdose of sanity is a kind of madness.

I suppose thinking you are God is crazy. Lethal, too. No society can tolerate God walking about in the streets, sitting in people's

houses, eating and drinking with them. So perhaps Caiaphas was right, in
a roundabout sort of way. Perhaps neither he nor I ever had any alternative but to kill Jesus off.

I keep telling myself that. I don't like killing good men, however
zany. But sometimes it's necessary. The only thing you can do. It's
for their good as much as for anyone else's. Because if you don't kill
them legally and with the due process of the law, somebody sooner or
later is going to organise a lynching party and do the job for you. And
then life really does get difficult.

Maybe it is just a rumour - this story that he's alive again.
Caiaphas says it is, and he's the religious expert. I hope to God he's
right. If he isn't, I'm finished. Not even a lawyer of your calibre could
get me off that kind of a hook. Perhaps I should resign while I can.
Pull out and let them get on with it their own way. Just put it all down
and pack up and walk away.

It's just that ..... Cass, what if he wasn't mad? What if he really
was God? Is God? What if the rumour is true and he really is back again,
alive in this city tonight? Politically, of course, we'd be back to
square one with a civil war on our hands. A struggle for power between
Rome and Jewish Nationalism. But oddly enough it isn't that I'm worried
about. What really troubles me is myself. How am I supposed to go on
living with the knowledge that God came to live in my Provinces and I had
him crucified?

Forgive me for troubling you with all this. Especially as there's
nothing you can do to help now. I don't need a good lawyer, after all.
What I need is a good psychiatrist.

Regards,

Portius Pilate

I have never trusted this man. His opinion of me
is a mirror-reflection of my opinion of him. Doesn't
the fool realise that without my support he wouldn't
last five minutes as Governor ?

PHOTOSTAT OF NOTE FOUND ON THE BODY OF
JUDAS SIMSON (KNOWN AS ISCARIOT), COMMITTED
SUICIDE 22.4.81.

SECRET

God forgive me, I did not do it for the money. I thought he was Messiah and wished only to force his hand. Make him declare himself in power and glory. Dear God, what have I done? I never meant him to die, only to

PHOTOCOPIED
DATE 27.4.81 — 09.45
SIGNED JRBooR (WPC 069)

M Nemeth D/Sgt

LETTER FROM JESUS BARABBAS TO SAM HANNAK INTERCEPTED APRIL 26
AND TRANSCRIBED DUE TO ILLEGIBILITY OF HANDWRITING.

Safe House 2

23.4.81

Dear Sam,

In case you haven't heard on the grapevine, I'm off the hook.
Full pardon from the Head Man, would you believe? I know, mate. I
don't believe it myself yet. It's true, all the same. This time
yesterday I was in the death cell waiting for the big drop. Now
I'm free.

It was a switch, see? They pulled in another guy to take my
place. Three executions booked and three guys got the chop. But
this other chap, he went instead of me. God knows why.

The word is he was innocent. Seems like those pious boot-
lickers in the Sanhedrin didn't go a bundle on him and they cooked
up this treason charge, flannelled the Governor rotten and ran
the poor guy up the hill in my place. But he was innocent. Not
a Freedom Fighter at all. Just one of those half-baked dreamers
with too much mouth and not enough muscle to make his dreams stick.
Bit of a religious fanatic, they say, in his own way. Jesus
Davidson. Been stumping the country these last three years. Now
he's bought it. Dead and buried, mate, same's I should've been.

And that's what gets me, Sam. That's why I feel so lousy.
Maybe it's just - y'know - reaction like. It's not every day you
eyeball death and he turns his head away first. I should be
jumping about, I know that. But I'm not. I feel like I've been
used, somehow. And that gets right up my nose.

This Jesus - who did he think he was, anyway? Dying up there
on Skull Hill in my place. My place. The way I see it, Sam, I
haven't cheated the gallows, I've been cheated myself.

You and me, mate, we're old hands at this Freedom Fighter
lark. We know the score. Have done ever since we dropped out of
the first year Social Science and started putting our ideas into

action. Drop a clanger in this game and you're out. Kaput.
Finished. Like it's a built-in risk, isn't it? Nobody wants it
to happen but at least it makes sense in a crazy sort of way.
We're in business to kill Romans. They're in business to kill
us. That's what it's all about, where it's at. Right?

But having some holier-than-thou country boy whose never
laid a mine or blown up a personnel carrier or cut a couple of
Roman throats in an alley - having him step in and take the
rap for you - well, that's not on, is it? I mean, how d'you
think I feel this morning, full of grub and damn-all to do but
enjoy myself - while he's wrapped up in a shroud in his grave?

OK, he brought it on himself. Shot his mouth off once
too often and got clobbered. Fair enough. He wasn't my style but
he must've had some bottle to get himself in Caiaphas's bad books.
I wouldn't have minded dying up there with a guy like that. I
mean, if you've gotta go, you've gotta go. It's him going and
me not - that's what I can't stomach somehow.

I dunno, Sam. All my life I've fought for freedom. The
chance to live my life without having to knuckle under to some
toffee-nosed Roman squaddie. Freedom to live - that's all that
matters,isn't it? What we've always said. But what about
freedom to die? This Jesus - he's robbed me of that. A milk-
and-water do-gooder who was all talk and no action. How can
a man hold his head up again if he's let somebody like that pay
the bill?

The thing is, Sam (and this is between you and me) I like
the sound of him. I know - he wasn't our sort. Too many
principles. Too damned honest. Playing this game with that
sort of background's like fighting with one hand tied behind
your back. But - well, there's something about the guy that
gets to me. I keep thinking if only we'd got together, say a
couple of years back. He was peaking then, see? Pulling the
crowds in, really telling it the way it was. All he needed was
a couple of thousand heavy men - and we could've laid them on,
no sweat. I mean, with his crowd-pulling and our muscle - man
we'd have had it made. Played our cards right, we'd have been

marching Pilate and Caiaphas up that hill long ago. As it is,
he's croaked, I'm a marked man and we're back to square one.

Let's face it, Sam, we need a guy like that. A front man
the crowds'll follow. They're too scared of us to back us up.
When it comes to the crunch, they'd rather have a bit of peace
and quiet and the money coming in regularly and Romans running
the show than be out on the streets pulling the place apart
with people like us. He could've been king, Sam. He had the
makings from all I hear. So why did he have to blow it? And
why, having blown it, did he have to shove me out and carry the
can for me? It's a liberty, Sam, that's what it is.A diabolical
liberty.

You know what they're saying here now? That he was God. I
know, I know, but that's what the word is. And they reckon he'll
be back. Pathetic, isn't it? You've seen what a man looks like
when he comes off the cross. Nobody comes back from that, mate.
Nobody.

It'd be something, though, wouldn't it, Sam? If he came
back. I wouldn't feel so bad about it then. Both of us,alive
- I could wear that. It's being alive when he's dead - that's
what I can't take.

                                        Barabbas

This one needs watching !

G.

Xth LEGION

THE IMPERIAL ROMAN ARMY

Private T. Denati,
C Comapny, 10th Legion,
Army of Occupation,
Israel.
APO.Box25/182/MEF

26.4.81

Now then girl,

By the time you get this I'll be on a trooper bound for
dere old Napoli. No,ducks, not posted and not on leave neither.
Out. Ive got me ticket,see. Sort of bought meself out, fourteen
years in the old regiment and now I'm for Civvy Street so how's
that for a bit of good news eh?

Like, I was on this death squad last Friday when three
pore devils got the chop bright and early and your everloving
detailed to do the honours. Nasty old job that is. I've been
on a few on my time and its always a lousey deal but its gotto be
done, if we dont show the flag now and then Gawd help us. We
live on a volcanoe out here, ducks and when you hear a bit of
a rumble like, well you get stuck in and do something about it
sharpish or else. And this was one hellava rumble. If youd seen
that mob eight deep on both sides of the street, struth it was
murder to hear them howling for blood like there was no tommorrow
as there wasnt for the three chums we was trotting up old Skull
Hill that morning.

Two of them was rubbish, tearaways full of aggro who called
themselves Freedom Fighters but they was just thuggs. Which was how they
behaived, cursing and shouting the odds all the way to the cross
both of them. But the third was differebt like,quiet sort of
bloke,not vialent just bonkers. Definately round the twist,
he was,thought he was king of the jews, like. Didn't look much of
a king, mind, not last Friday morning, more like a scarecrow tham
a king by the time we got through with him. Countyy boy from
one of the little villages up north, out of his depth in the
city you could see that. Been on his feet all night, tried
by the Sannhedrine that the local jewish court,ducks and then
by the governer, flogged ad teazed and gennerally mucked about,

time he get to the cross he was three parts agoner already

    Still, maaleesh that as we say out here, you don't want
to hear about him do you. Only the thing is one of the perks
onthe death squad is you get to collect a few duds like cos we
strips 'em, see, before we nale them up and anything their wearing
we sort out between us and flog it next day down the Flea Market
I know it sounds a bit rough, ducks but there aint no sence in
wasting good clobber is there? I mean they dont need nothing like
that where there going.

Not that theres much to flog most times, the criminal classes
over here arent what youd call famous for there turnout, like
two of them we chopped last Friday. Just rags they had woudnt
even make a.decant duster. But the third guy, the quiet one had
one of them pesant robes, nice bit of homespun all puer wool
and handsewn, weaved in one peice see? Bit of a local craft like
Some of the lads buy them and send them home to their old ladies
for dressing gowns, reel cosy on a winters night when their old
mans away overseas fighting for emperor and country

    Anyways we had a look at this one and it was OK apart from
a few bloodstanes which woud wash out, only there was three
of us on the squad wasnt their , and three into one wont go

Old,lofty the corporal in charge was all for ripping in into
three lenths but I didnt see the sebce in that so in the end
we chucked dice for it and who won? Dead right, ducks
your everloving husband , didnt I? Now dont go getting
exited cos I wont be bringing it back.

    We polished them off about 15.00 hours two of them anyways
the quiet one was dead alreddy, slipped away while we was dicing
for his robes So we got them down and sent the crowd
packing, not that they needed much telling for once cos there
holey day startsaat sunset on a Friday and they were all
dead keen to get home and have a wash and brushup before
nipping along to church to say there praires which is nice
innit when youve spent the day watching three geezers croak
slowly and then pop off and ask God to make you a good boy tomorrow,
well thats religon for you.

I was back in baracks half thinking about giving
that robe a bit of a dhobi before going down to the wet
canteen to wash the taste of the day out of me throte when
the sarge comes in and says theirs a geezer wants to xgxksee
me like. A civvy he was, old codger, looked about a
hundred and four, rich an all you could see that, said his
name was Joseff from Arimathea which is a little fly blown
dump just up the road apiece from Jerusalem which is a
biggef fly blown dump just down the road from Arima whetsisname.
I asked him what he wanted and he said it was the robe, oh
he didnt come out with it just like that they never do these
boys not when they want something reel bad, but thats what
he was after, the pesants robe. I asked him why, cos if you
had seen him, ducks, the way he was dressed and that there
was no way he was going to ware it. Anyway he tetters about
abit and then says he was an oppo of this Jesus Davidson
but in secret like. A bit twitched he was kept looking over
his sholder and dogeing about frightened of there own shadoes
some of them wogs.

    Seems like this Jesus the quiet one of the three was very
religous and holey, went about doing good and that, healing
people and working mirracles, no harm in that of course only he
got mixed up in politicks see? Got this idea he was a king
which is definately not on here, angways this old geezer keeps
on about how wonderfull he was and what a crime it was to chop
him as hed never done nobody no harm all his life. I got a
bit brassed off with him and said OK mate, so what do you want
me to do about him get him back from the dead or something?
Which shook him a bit. He got very uptight and started
waiving his arms about the way they do out here very
comical to watch it is. Look I said Ive had a herd day
mate. Cut the cackle and come to the point right? So
he said could he have the robe as a sooveneer like.

    So then it was my turn to box clever, I cracked on it was
a bit of good stuff, hardly worn and said, You want it its going
to cost you mate. And stood by to haggle which is something
they do very well here. But not this old geexer, he fishes out
a lether bag all nice and heavy and says, Theres a couple of
hundred here, will that do? Id have taken twentyfive which is
twice what Id have got down the market, but he was all of a
twitch so I sort of hung back a bit and sure enough out comes
another bag. He says, four hundred then. I grinned and said,
Make in five and its yours. Only he didnt have another century
on him and scratched about in his pocketts and russelled up
another forty seveh and I said OK seeing how its you mate. And
got the robe and handed it over.

Four hundred and forty seven nicker ducks, how about that.
I put mename on the Company Commanders list to see the Adj next
morning and slept with the loot in a belt next me skin. So there
we are ducks, the Adj marched me in to see the CO and I payed
on the nale, a hundred and twenty quid and I was a free man
plus a travel warrent back to Napoli and a nice little nest
egg in me belt for when I get home. The Colonel was a bit
suspishous, wanted to know where Id got the gelt from so
I spun him a yarn about being a bit lucky on the geegees, he
didnt beleive a word of it but what could he do? He made me
wate twenty four hours in case some guy reported a theft and
then signed the papers and shook hands with me for the first
and last time. I'm on the boat in the morning ducks, be with
you in a couple of weeks no sweat. And then ....

    Funny reelly innit the way the cookie crumbles, I mean
who woud have thought going on a death squad woud buy me me
freedom? They reckon thats what he was on about most of the
time, this Jesus chap, said hed come to set the people free,
said he was going to die so they could live in freedom. This
lot, some hopes, we're in controll here and there in the gutter
same as theyve always been and and always will be, its going
to take more than a mixed up carpenters son to change the world
as they will find out. Still changed my world ducks and yours.
Next time your near a church nip in an say a praire for him
will you, cant do no harm can it? I mean theres nothing wrong
with religon in its proper place in church. Its when you drag
it out in the street and start shooting your mouth off about it
you find yourself up the creek without a paddel, same as he did.

    Ah well, ducks, like the man said its an ill wind.

        SWALK

        Titus
        XXX

DEPT Y   **ROOM** 401

ISRAELI POLICE headquarters

King David Sq
Jerusalem WI

MEMORANDUM   for Internal circulation only

From   Chief Inspector S M Jacobs   **Ref** JD/45/MM7
           Y Department

To   Commander Z B Thompson   **Date** 27 April
           MC CRE

Sir

The enclosed transcript represents one half of a telephone
conversation recorded 09.23 hours, April 25. Unfortunately,
due to a malfunction of the monitoring device plugged into
the telephone itself, the other half of the conversation
was not picked up, although we have been able to identify
the person receiving the call (as you will note). The
recording was in fact obtained through the back-up audio
bug previously installed in the room.

S M Jacobs CI

CLASSIFIED

ISRAELI POLICE

TRANSCRIPT OF TELEPHONE CONVERSATION
RECORDED 09.23 Hours   DATE April 25

SECRET

ORIGIN OF CALL: 051-44-3276

ADDRESS: Top Flat, 7 Chain Street, Jerusalem S1

CALLER'S NAME: Mary Magdalene (Miss), known as 'the Magdala'. Sometime
                    hostess at the Red Stocking Cabaret, Solomon Street,
                    Jerusalem EC2

CONNECTION: Number not traced. Believed to be Martha Magdalene (Miss),
                    sister of caller. Present address: Vine Cottage, Main
                    Road, Bethany.

TRANSCRIPT READS:

MARY M: Hullo, Martha? Mary here ..... Oh, I'm fine. On top of the
            world, dear ..... Yes, I know, but that's all changed now.
            He's come back, just as he said he would and ..... Jesus, of
            course ..... Yes he's alive again. Isn't it ..... No dear,
            not a rumour, I've seen him and so has Peter and some of the
            others. Seen him, talked to him ..... No, I'm not, dear.
            Excited, yes. Overjoyed. But not hysterical ..... In the
            garden by the tomb where we ..... Yesterday morning early.
            We went to give him a proper burial, Joanna and Salome and a
            couple of other women. There'd not been time, you see on
            Friday before the Sabbath began. I mean we weren't prepared
            or anything and the soldiers were in such a hurry to get him
            into the tomb and seal it up and mount the guard ..... Yes, a
            guard, dear, didn't you know? Anyway, we set out at first
            light with spices and fresh ointments and a new shroud. Oh,
            Martha, it sounds so foolish now, a bunch of weeping women
            going off to give him a decent funeral, but at the time we
            thought it was the least we could do for him. All we could
            do ..... I know dear, that's what Salome said going into the
            garden. 'How're we going to shift that big stone and get
            inside?' ..... We didn't have to. When we got to the tomb it
            was open and the soldiers gone ..... No, dear, no damage. The

seal had been broken of course when the stone was removed,
but otherwise everything was quite normal, except that the
tomb was empty. Well, not quite empty because his shroud
was there and the head-cloth, but no body, no Jesus .....
That's what we thought, of course. Grave-robbers. I felt
sick, I really did, Martha. I mean, as if killing him
wasn't enough they couldn't even let him rest in peace
after all he'd done for so many, all his kindness and
understanding, all the love he'd given us. I imagined him
bundled into a ditch somewhere, or thrown on the rubbish
tip in the Hinnon gorge where they throw the murderers
after execution. Oh, it was awful. Absolute desolation
..... I wish you had been too, dear, especially when he
came and ..... No, I was quite alone then. The others
had gone back to tell the men, but I stayed there in the
garden just outside the tomb. I was weeping and shaking -
in a terrible state. Well you know how much I loved him,
and I just felt there was nothing left to go on living for.
I just wanted to die there ..... Yes, I know, dear, but
you've always been the practical one, haven't you? So much
stronger than me ..... What? ..... Oh, well I suddenly
heard this man's voice asking me why I was crying and I
turned round and there was a vague figure standing there.
The sun was up and behind him and my eyes were blurred
with tears and I didn't know who he was, unless perhaps
the gardener. I remember I asked him if he knew about the
grave robbers, if he knew where they'd taken Jesus. I was
terribly confused, you see. All churned up inside. But
then he said my name. 'Mary', he said, quietly, gently with
just a hint of laughter in his voice - as if he was excited
and happy and - oh, bubbling over with a huge, wonderful
secret he was bursting to share with somebody. And of
course I knew then it was him. I mean nobody has ever said
my name the way he does. And I shook my head and rubbed my
eyes and stared at him and he moved a little to one side
and the sun shone on his face and it was Jesus ..... No,
dear, no mistake. I know what you're thinking. I'm a
dreamer, head in the clouds, romantic. I know that. You're
thinking: She's seen somebody like him. She wants him back
more than anything in the world and she's seen a young man
with a beard and she thinks it's Jesus Davidson ..... Oh,
I don't blame you, dear. Not for one moment. But it isn't
like that, it truly isn't. I saw him there. I saw the wounds
in his hands and feet and the scratches from the thorns on
his forehead and I saw his face, glowing with life and health

and ..... Because he's God, Martha, that's how. I know
that for certain now and because he's alive, I'm alive
too. Really alive, the way I've never been before .....
Oh, Martha, I'm not going to hide behind that silly
hostess title any more. I was a prostitute and you know
it. All right I'm not one now, haven't been since he
first spoke to me two years ago, but in the eyes of most
men that's what I am, and always will be. And God got
up out of his grave yesterday morning and came to me first.
Isn't it marvellous? ..... Oh, but they have, Martha.
Peter and John - all of them have seen him now, except
Thomas. He wasn't with us, poor lad, and he's very, very
hard to convince ..... What? ..... No, not in the garden
dear, later here in the flat ..... Yes, we were all here
having supper yesterday evening. I'd wanted to rush out
and grab everybody I met and tell them he was alive again,
but Peter and John both said it would be foolish. The
rumour's all over the city of course, and they said Caiaphas
would be livid and could turn ugly and we'd better stay put
for a day or two till we saw how things were going. So we
were up here with all the doors locked and he - well, he
just came in, Martha, through the locked door, one moment
he wasn't there, the next he was standing in the room,
smiling ..... That's exactly what they thought. It was a
terrible shock, of course. I mean, I'd seen him already
but they hadn't. They only had my word for it and to see
him actually there in the flesh really bowled them over and
they thought he was a ghost ..... No, dear, he wasn't. Ghosts
don't eat fish suppers, do they? But he did. Held out his
hands and we all saw the cruel nail wounds and he said, 'I'd
like a little supper, please.' I gave him a plate and a fork
and he stood there eating, calm as you please. 'Very good,'
he said and smiled at Peter. 'Almost as good as the fish you
catch, Peter.' And that did it, of course. No more doubts,
no more fears either. He was just himself, you see, dear,
our Jesus the way we remembered him, the way we loved him.
Oh, Martha darling, I wish you'd been with us then. It
was such a party we had. You know how he always loved eating
out with friends, what good company he always was and how
the Pharisees hated him for it. Well it was like that only
more so, if you see what I mean? ..... Prayers, dear? No
we didn't say any prayers. We just had a wonderful happy
meal together ..... But it wasn't like that, Martha. Not a
solemn affair not religious at all in that old-fashioned
sense ..... Well, I'm sorry, but if you'd been there .....

Martha, look, you remember that story he told once, about
the son who went away and came back home and his father
laid on a special dinner for him - music and food and wine
and laughter and how the father said, 'This my son was
dead and is alive again'? Well it was just like that, dear
just exactly like that ..... No, he didn't. We wanted to
of course. After supper we assumed he would stay the night,
be with us all the time. But he didn't ..... I don't know,
dear. There's something different about him. I mean, he's
the same Jesus but there's something more, a sort of extra
dimension I suppose. A bit uncanny, really - or perhaps
that's just us trying to adjust to a dead man being alive
again. But I don't think it's that, not altogether. He's
come into his own, y'see. Won the battle and moved into
his kingdom. Perhaps that's it. Perhaps now, for the
first time since we've known him, he's really himself at
last ..... I don't know that either, dear. We're all going
north tomorrow so I won't be seeing you for a while yet,
I'm afraid ..... Yes, of course dear. I'll let you know as
soon as I can. But you're not to worry about me. Nobody
can hurt us now or stop us telling the good news. Not
Caiaphas or Pilate or anybody. Jesus is back, alive again,
with us for always. That's all that matters ..... Bless
you, dear, I will. You take care, too ..... Yes, as soon
as I can ..... Goodbye dear.

TRANSCRIPT ENDS

So this is the source of the rumour. We must find
a way to silence this woman as quickly as possible
— but who would credit a 'Messiah' who
associates with her kind ?

6.

REF PA/CT/14

25.4.81

Office of the Temple Commissioners
PALACE YARD,
JERUSALEM

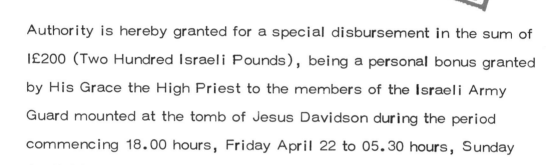

Authority is hereby granted for a special disbursement in the sum of I£200 (Two Hundred Israeli Pounds), being a personal bonus granted by His Grace the High Priest to the members of the Israeli Army Guard mounted at the tomb of Jesus Davidson during the period commencing 18.00 hours, Friday April 22 to 05.30 hours, Sunday April 24.

This bonus is an ex gratia payment made in recognition of the special hazards faced by the guards in consequence of the earth tremor recorded at 05.12 hours on April 24 which burst open the tomb and made it possible for the body of Davidson to be removed by grave robbers.

A.T.Zehcrias F.I.C.A.
Chief Accountant.

The men in question have been instructed to spread the grave-robbing story as widely as possible. If, as I hope, this establishes it in the public mind, it will be money well spent.

Caiaphas

THE ROYAL PALACE

HIS GRACE THE LORD CAIAPHAS,
THE PALACE,
JERUSALEM,

26/4/81

Your Grace,

I write this with some diffidence and considerable regret.
As you know, I have been your Personal Assistant now for
almost twelve years and have considered it a privilege to
be so employed. It is therefore only after a great deal
of thought and heart-searching that I write now resigning
my position. It has not been an easy decision to make
but I feel that I have no choice.

It would be discourteous of me not to give at least some
indication of my reasons for making this decision, but
it is difficult to do this without seeming to cause offence.
That is not my intention and I hope you will accept what
I have to say in the spirit in which it is offered.

The fact is, sir, that last Thursday evening something
happened to me which I can neither explain nor forget.
You will recall that on your instructions I accompanied
the men who were sent that night to Gethsemane to apprehend
Jesus Davidson - Jesus of Nazareth as he is popularly called.

Let me emphasise that I went very willingly, since at that
time I shared Your Grace's view of this man - that he was a
blasphemer and a threat to the safety of the nation.

Arresting a man is never a pleasant task, but I went fully
persuaded that it was my duty to be there on that occasion as
your personal representative. I have often observed Your
Grace's anxiety and distress brought about by Davidson's
defiance of our sacred Law and by his persistent attacks upon
the Church - and indeed upon yourself. I went to Gethsemane
with a sense of thankfulness that at last he was to be
silenced.

As was reported at the trial, Davidson and his men offered
little resistance to the arresting squad. In fact, I was the
only casualty. I was attacked by one of Davidson's followers
who swung his sword at me, caught me a glancing blow on the
side of the head and severed my left ear. I had a moment of
shock and blinding pain and would have fallen had not Jesus
himself gripped my arm and held me upright. I heard him say
something like, 'That's enough, lads'. And then he touched my
head with his fingertips and to my utter astonishment my ear
was back in place and completely sound and undamaged. There
was no pain; only a warm, not unpleasant sensation - a kind
of tingling feeling.

Before I could begin to thank him it was too late. He was
seized by the soldiers and hustled away to stand trial before
you. Much of what happened subsequently I found both con-
fusing and horrifying. I do not, of course, presume to
question Your Grace's superior knowledge and wisdom for I am
sure you acted for the best, as you saw it. But I found the
whole affair - the trial and the execution - extremely

upsetting. I cannot forget the look **of** compassion on his face as he held me, the gentleness of his hand as he healed me, and now I find it impossible to believe that such a man could be an enemy of Israel, much less of God.

Your Grace, it is not only that he performed a miracle of healing although that in itself would give me cause to ponder, but also that he displayed such extraordinary compassion. The healing itself was miraculous. The motive behind it - the love and concern of which it was the symbol - this I find no words to describe.

I do not begin to understand the rumours of his re-appearance three days after his burial. You have said that they are totally untrue; that his friends robbed the grave, hid his body and deliberately spread the lie of his resurrection. My instinct is to agree with you, for how can a man come back from the grave?

Yet I find myself remembering those moments of confusion and terror in Gethsemane. I see Judas Iscariot betraying his friend with a kiss of greeting. I see the anger on the faces of the men around Jesus, the quick flash of the sword blade in the light of the torches. I feel again that sudden pain, the warm blood on my neck, the grip of his hand on my arm. All this is vividly etched on my mind, as real now as when it happened. But it fades into obscurity against the remembered touch of his healing fingers, the sense of power flowing out of him into the very tissue and substance of my flesh. And I keep asking myself what kind of man was this who in the moment of his greatest peril found time to heal an enemy?

I don't know the answer to that, Your Grace; only that, right or wrong, something inside me insists that there was more in Jesus Davidson than perhaps we understood. If this is so, I fear a terrible mistake has been made. They are saying in the city now that he was God and that that is why death could not hold him in the grave. But how can God live as a man among us, Your Grace? How can he die on a cross? I take leave to doubt, with respect, that even your deep theological learning can answer those questions. And yet, who but God can replace a severed ear with the touch of his hand? And who but God can love as this man loved?

Feeling as I do, it is clearly impossible for me to remain in your employ. I have nothing but respect for your abilities and for the devotion with which you have always served the Church in your exalted capacity. Such ability and devotion deserves only the most loyal and single-minded service and this I am no longer able to give. My continued presence as your Personal Assistant would only cause you embarrassment. This, at least, I can spare you. Accordingly I regretfully offer my resignation to take place with immediate effect.

Please believe me, Your Grace, when I say how hard it is for me to write as I have written. It has always been both a pleasure and a privilege to serve you. I am truly sorry it has to end this way.

Your obedient servant.

A bitter blow indeed!
I trusted this man implicitly.

B. Malchus.

DEPARTMENT OF INTERNAL SECURITY   "Shalom", 22 Long Row, Arimathea

30th April '81

My dear Hannah,

I hesitate to impose upon our long friendship in this way but you've always been good enough to listen to my little problems and advise me.   Very good advice, too, as I remember with gratitude.   So I venture to write to you now about Jesus Davidson of Nazareth who was recently executed on a treason charge.   As you know I have been interested in him for some time now - fascinated by him is perhaps a better way of putting it.   It has seemed to me quite remarkable that a man with no real qualifications or credentials - the son of a village carpenter - could say and do the astonishing things he has said and done.

To be perfectly frank, he frightened me more than a little for his thinking was so clear, so right - and at the same time so revolutionary.   I found myself agreeing with him, welcoming his ministry, yet fearful to come out into the open and support him, which was cowardly of me I suppose.   But I'm an old man and no longer able to bear the stress of involvement in the life and purpose of so charismatic a personality.   I could see that he was bound to draw unfavourable attention to himself in high places, and I wanted no part of the inevitable crisis.

I made that very clear to my colleagues in the Sanhedrin. Whenever he was discussed I took no part in the debate and when, at the end, we voted on his guilt or innocence I abstained.   Not that it would have made any difference had I had the courage to vote for his acquittal.   The verdict against him was overwhelming, a triumph for His Grace the High Priest.   I accepted that verdict albeit unhappily.   It seemed to me the whole affair of his arrest and trial was far too hurried and in my view the witnesses against him put up a very poor showing.   Indeed it was only when he himself declared that he was Messiah that we were able to proceed to a conviction.

No, I was not happy about it, but in the circumstances I could see no way in which I could vote against it. Blasphemy, after all, is a cardinal offence and as His Grace said, whoever God is he is not the son of a carpenter from Nazareth. The subsequent charge of treason was, I believe, a purely political matter; a lever to force the hand of the Governor-General who alone can pronounce the death sentence. I have no qualms at all about not voting for that. What I do have is this strange feeling of obligation to Jesus, as if somewhere along the line there would be some act only I could do to help him. What that was only became clear to me after his execution. A shocking affair, brutally cruel and, I firmly believe, unjust. I was there Hannah, that Friday on Skull Hill. I witnessed the whole degrading spectacle and when he died I suddenly knew my moment had come.

I hope I am making this clear to you, my dear. The trouble these days is that I tend to get muddled sometimes, express myself badly. But in my own mind it is all quite clear now. It had been a shattering day. An eclipse at noon, a fairly severe earth tremor and an act of despicable vandalism in the Temple where someone ripped the curtain in front of the Holy and Holies from top to bottom. In the aftermath of all this the soldiers were ordered to break the legs of the three crucified men so that they would die and could be disposed of before the Sabbath began. Jesus himself was already dead, so he was spared this final, cruel indignity, but when his followers got him down off the cross they were quite at a loss to know what to do with the body. Which was when I made my offer.

Some years ago I purchased a tomb in a garden behind Skull Hill. This was now made available to them for Jesus; too

little too late, perhaps, but at least it was something and
when they accepted I was filled with a kind of peace.   I was
probably easing my conscience when it was safe to do so, but
the thought of him lying where one day I hope to lie pleased, and
in a way comforted me.   Whatever else I had failed to do, I had
at least done this; a final act of recognition and sympathy.
Only it was not final.   My tomb is empty again.   Jesus Davidson
broke out of it three days after his death and has been reported
alive in the city, seen by his friends who have spoken with him and
shared a meal with him.   I know it is quite impossible, but the
fact remains that they are convinced he is alive again and the
tomb - my tomb - is certainly empty.

I have not seen Jesus myself.   I can hardly expect to, for
why should he seek out a man who did nothing for him while he was
alive?   But those who have seen him are adamant about it and quite
transformed with joy, totally oblivious to the danger they are in.
And they are in danger for the High Priest is said to be extremely
angry - and I suspect not a little anxious, for if Jesus is truly
risen, His Grace's position is to say the least an invidious one.
But is mine any better?   I very much fear I have been more than
usually foolish.   They are saying Jesus is God you see, and whatever
sort of gift you make to God it isn't a tomb.   Apparently when
Jesus was born three Eastern sages brought him Messianic gifts.
It was left to a foolish old man to mark his death with the gift
of a tomb, the implication of which being that he was no Messiah.
I do not consider myself to be an expert theologian but even I know
that Messiah cannot die.   And yet, Jesus died.

I have a small confession to make to you, Hannah.   When Jesus
died I bought his robe off one of the soldiers who carried out the
execution.   I did it on impulse, feeling that I wanted some sort
of memento of him, something of his to keep and cherish.   I have
it here in the house but I cannot bear to look at it for it mocks

my lack of faith in him; a souvenir of a dead man who is
no longer dead.   I find it very disturbing somehow for it
seems now to symbolise an attitude of mind which is quite
wrong; a looking back to God when we should be looking forward.
It's all of a piece with my gift of the tomb, of course.   Was
it an act of faith, a declaration, however late in the day, that
I believed him to be what he claimed to be that night in front
of the Sanhedrin?   Or was it merely an act of pity, or worse
still, of denial?   Do we really want a God who lives among us?
Are we not much happier to have him safely locked away in a
church or a tomb, revered, worshipped but not really accepted
as a part of life?

     I fear I am very confused.   Can you give me your counsel?
A few wise words to ease my bewilderment, my sense of having
somehow missed the whole point.   I hope you can, Hannah, I
hope you can.   It is not the most comforting thing to have
met the Lord of Life and given him a tomb.

             Yours,

Joseph

*Make sure this man never sits
in the Sanhedrin again.*

C.

From   Lieutenant Q.A. Geller
        A Company

Xth LEGION

THE IMPERIAL ROMAN ARMY

MEMORANDUM

Date   April 26

To   Colonel P.L. Macer, M.C., D.S.O.
       Officer Commanding 10th Legion
       Jerusalem

Sir,

    With reference to my request to see you on a personal matter (April 23)
I am commanded by the Adjutant formally to state the nature of this matter
and to provide you with written details. This I now have the honour to do.

    In accordance with A Company's DRO's (Friday, April 22) I commanded
the Execution Squad charged with the crucifixion of three criminals convicted of treason against the State and the person of His Imperial Majesty,
Tiberius Caesar. The executions to take place publicly on Skull Hill that
same morning.

    In spite of a major public demonstration, the executions were carried
out successfully and without incident. I would like, in this connection,
sir, to commend the members of the squad, and in particular CSM Valens,
for exemplary conduct and efficiency in what was a potentially dangerous
situation. From first to last they performed their duty in a manner which
brought credit to the regiment.

    There were, sir, as you will recall, certain features of this
execution assignment which were unusual. Notably the eclipse of the sun
at noon that day and a moderate/severe earth tremor centred half a mile
north-east of the city wall. This combination of natural phenomena was
associated in the public mind with the death of one of the criminals -
Jesus Davidson, the so-called King of the Jews. It is about this man
and the manner of his dying that I wish to speak to you, sir.

    I am no stranger to crucifixions and have learned by experience
what to expect. Two of the men executed last Friday reacted to the
ordeal in predictable fashion. One of them maintained a stoical silence.
The other railed and cursed at us from the cross. But the third man -
Jesus - behaved quite differently. He was, I understand, a religious man.
Perhaps that is why he prayed on the cross, although this in itself is more or
or less SOP with those who profess a faith. What was unusual was the kind
of prayers Jesus used. They were - allowing for the fact that he was in

acute pain - not so much prayers as conversations with his God. A God he addressed as Father. More than that, in some involved way, he appeared to identify with his God - a father/son relationship which was so confused that it was difficult to determine, at times, which was which. As if, sir, he and his Father God were - well, one person.

It was perhaps, the agony he was suffering which blurred the issue. At one point he appeared to think his Father had deserted him - left him to die alone. Yet later, at the point of death, he committed himself to that same Father in an act of absolute trust and confidence.

He also - and this was most unusual - pleaded with his God to forgive us for his death.

I do not consider myself to be a sentimental man, sir. I have served eight years in the 10th, including active service in Gaul and North Africa, and such experience does not breed sentimentality. Nor am I a particularly religious man - although I believe in the existence of a God. As the Padre is fond of reminding us, religion is a good thing in its proper place. A support for our sense of duty, but never a hindrance to our fulfilling that duty. Until now I have not found that unreasonable. God in church and the Colonel (if you'll allow me to say so, sir, with respect) on parade. No problem. No conflict of loyalties. Until now.

Since last Friday I have been haunted by this man Jesus. I cannot get him - or the words he spoke on the cross - out of my mind. I was moved at the time to comment on his courage and his faith. When he died , the CSM said to me 'Something a bit odd about that one, sir.' I agreed. There was something odd about him. Something different. Something, as I now believe, uncanny.

I have taken the trouble to look up his record, sir. Mainly to satisfy myself that he was justly brought to trial and condemned. The evidence of his treasonable activities seem to me to be very thin indeed. The evidence of his deeply religious convictions, on the other hand, is impressive. There is a rumour going round the barracks that His Excellency, Lord Pilate, was not entirely con-vinced of his guilt and signed the death warrant only under protest. I have, of course, stamped on this rumour very firmly indeed. I put two men on a charge yesterday for spreading it in A Company. This I believe to be my duty as a loyal officer. In any event, what has been done has been done and cannot be altered now.

It is not the question of his guilt as a traitor that bothers
me, sir. It is the whole question of his identity. He would not
be the first innocent man to go to the cross. But I am increasingly
worried by the fact that he was perhaps more than that. Not just
an innocent man. Not even just a man.

I can well imagine with what impatience you will read this,
sir. Which is why I requested a personal interview. However, the
Adjutant, very properly insists that I proceed through the usual
channels.

Sir, there is another rumour abroad in the city now. Not a
piece of barrack-room gossip this time. It emanates from the Jewish
people themselves. This time last week I would have dismissed it
as being wishful thinking on the part of the followers of Jesus of
Nazareth. A desperate, rather pathetic attempt on their part to
justify their faith in him. But now I find myself unable to do so.

Sir, they are saying - and with immense conviction - that he
is alive again. They claim not only to have seen him but also to
have talked with him and even eaten a meal with him. And they are
saying now that he is God.

I have tried to dismiss this from my mind. But I am haunted
by his behaviour on the cross. By that curiously muddled, but
utterly convincing, conversation he had with - with whom? His
Father? Himself? I don't know. I don't understand how God can
be a man, how he can be crucified and buried. Much less how he
can return from the grave alive. But I find myself unable to
rationalise it, to explain it away. I suppose, sir, in a word,
I have begun to believe in him as - well, as God.

This being so, I clearly cannot continue in the Service. A
man with divided loyalties is in no position to command his fellows
even on garrison duty, let alone on active service. I understand that
- and its implications. The Army has been my life and I have not,
until now, ever for one moment considered any other. So it is with
a sense of deep regret that I ask you now to allow me to resign my
commission.

I have no idea at all what I shall do or where I shall go.
My instinct is to seek out some of the followers of Jesus and try
to learn more about this way of life which I understand he propounded.
But whether or not they will accept me is, of course, another matter.
It is asking a great deal to expect them to welcome into their company

the man in charge of the soldiers who actually killed their
leader. I can but try. They are said to base their philosophy
(if that's the right word) on forgiveness. And this is what I
need.

Sir, believe me when I say that I have not reached this
decision lightly. I have discussed it with the Adjutant and
the Padre, both of whom have urged me to reconsider. The
Adjutant has offered me home leave to give me time to sort myself
out. I appreciate this - and the fact that he assures me you
would be co-operative. But this is not something to be resolved
by a change of scenery. I would be as haunted by this man in
Italy as I am here in Jerusalem.

I have the honour, therefore, to request a personal interview
with you in order that I may resign my commission forthwith.

Q.A.Geller.

Quintus Geller. Lieutenant.

Superstitious rubbish.

ISRAELI POLICE
headquarters

Form AW/256/IPJ

28/1

King David Sq
Jerusalem WI

DEPARTMENT
OF INTERNAL
· SECURITY ·

W A R R A N T   T O   A R R E S T

NAME	Simon (alias Peter) Johnson
OCCUPATION	Fisherman (unemployed)
ADDRESS	7, Chain Street, Jerusalem S1
CHARGE	Treason
ISSUED TO	Rabbi Saul Troax, attached Special Squad
DATE	21.6.81
ISSUED BY	T P Matthews, Commisioner

T.P. Matthews

Issued on the express authority of His Grace the High Priest, this is a top priority warrant. Johnson's inflamatory speech in the Temple Court at the Feast of Weeks makes him the most wanted man in the dissident group claiming the return of Jesus Davidson to continue his subversive activities against Church and State. It is imperative that he be arrested and silenced immediately

TPM

THE ROYAL PALACE
THE OFFICE OF THE HIGH PRIEST

His Excellency the Governor,
The Residency,
Jerusalem.

21 June '81

Your Excellency,

Thank you for your note this morning. I hasten to
send you reassuring news.

Following the disturbance in the Temple court yesterday
morning during the celebration of the Feast of Weeks, I
have taken immediate action to contain the incident and
bring those concerned to book. You will appreciate that
this is not an easy task with the city crowded with visitors
and pilgrims, nor one which will quickly be accomplished.
I feel the poison is much more widely dispersed than I
feared. The whole country is tainted with it and it will
take time to eradicate it completely. But this I am
determined to do and have made all the necessary arrangements
to apprehend not only the ring-leaders but also any person,
of whatever standing, who can be proved to be involved. It
will, inevitably, put a great deal of pressure on our
prisons and add a considerable burden to our already over-
stretched police force. But I have appointed a man of

great tenacity and deep religious fervour to be in charge
of the operation. I confidently expect results within the
next few days.

I am, as ever, grateful to Your Excellency for so
willingly offering the assistance of the 10th Legion. I
hope very much it will not come to that. But it is comforting to have so practical a demonstration of your
support and concern. It is in times of crisis like these
that the good relations which exist between us are
particularly gratifying. Church and State together, and
of one mind, make a formidable weapon against insurrection.

You ask me for some explanation of the disturbance.
Let me assure you that it had nothing whatsoever to do
with the Feast of Weeks celebration. This, as you know,
is our early summer Feast at which we remember the giving
of the Law on Sinai and also hold a kind of early harvest
festival. Unlike some of our Feasts, which I freely admit
have certain political undertones, the Feast of Weeks is
a purely religious occasion - a time of thanksgiving and
praise.

What happened yesterday took us all by surprise. It
concerned, I'm sorry to say, our old adversary Jesus
Davidson. Not, I hasten to say, in the flesh this time.
His followers tried that particular ploy three days after
his crucifixion in April. Without success, as I'm sure you
will agree. A wild and foolish rumour and one which was
bound to find little sympathy. I have naturally kept my

ear close to the ground since then. Precautions are,
after all, cheap and sometimes rewarding. However, I was
satisfied from my agents' reports that the whole unfortunate
episode had been forgotten. Thanks in no small measure
to Your Excellency's quick and firm support, the Jesus
incident was closed.

Until yesterday morning. It now appears to have been
festering undergroung and to have emerged again, this time
in a different, and potentially more dangerous, form.
His followers are now claiming that he has returned to
them. Not as a man of flesh and blood but as a spirit.
The word has a number of connotations, the most popular
of which is a ghost - in this case, disgustingly enough -
a holy ghost. But that is not to say Jesus has appeared
to them in some insubstantial manifestation. They claim
that his energy, his power - his essence, if you like - has
been given to them. His spirit, in other words, fragmented
and dispersed among those who believe in him.

Superstitious rubbish, of course. And blasphemous in
the extreme. But we both know how prone the population is
to this kind of thing, how eager to accept the supernatural.
I suppose it is inevitable, considering the miserable lives
most of them lead - which is not in any way to be interpreted
as a slur on Your Excellency's clement and just administration.
And, as I think you will appreciate, it is difficult to
combat. A man you can track down, arrest and execute (as we
did in April). But a spirit - an idea involving both heart
and head - this is something much more elusive.

Already the story is being embroidered. Bazaar gossip
has it that the men who were closest to Jesus were gathered
in the upper room of a house in Chain Street, just south of
the Temple court. People are saying that the house quite
suddenly caught fire. But not in the normal way. One
moment it was there, just one house in a row of terraced
houses. The next it was an inferno - flames leaping all
round it, inside and out, shooting out of the windows,
leaping up through the roof. Flames, no smoke. A kind
of white-hot fury of fire which enveloped the house, whilst
leaving those on either side completely untouched. The
men in the house were seen at the windows - or so it is
said - with the fire blazing not only round them but also
within them. Bursting out of their bodies. Flaring in
their eyes and hair. Ridiculous, of course.

As is the story that the fire disappeared as suddenly
as it had arrived, leaving the house itself intact and
undamaged in any way - not so much as a smoke stain - and
the men inside unscathed. Only the very gullible would
countenance such an obvious fabrication. But I'm afraid
we have more than our share of those in the city just now
- villagers up from the country, illiterate peasants, dull-
witted and open to any superstition, the wilder the better.

It is being said in certain quarters (which will bear
watching closely) that the fire was in reality the Shekinah
of God. I cannot begin to tell you how deeply this offends
me. The Shekinah - the glory - of God is a very rare
phenomenon. Very rare indeed. It has heralded some
religious event of immense significance for our people.

It was seen by Moses in the desert as he prepared himself
to lead the nation out of Egypt. On that occasion it
flared in a bush, burning fiercely for several minutes,
but leaving the bush unharmed. It appeared in the sky at
the Exodus, leading the people across the desert wastes
in safety. It blazed on the summit of Sinai when the Law
was given to Moses - indeed, it glowed in his face when he
returned to the camp. I mention all these instances at the
risk of boring you, in order that you may appreciate the
utter absurdity of the claim that it was this same Shekinah
which enveloped the house in Chain Street yesterday morning.
Nothing could be further from the truth - or in worse taste.
Such a pernicious statement is on a par with the stories
that the Shekinah appeared outside the tomb in which Jesus
Davidson was buried; that it was seen by his followers on
the Mount of Olives when he is **said** to have ascended into
heaven after his supposed resurrection. Even that it was
observed in the sky over Bethlehem the night he was born -
on that occasion, would you believe, accompanied by a
heavenly choir!

You will see how little credence can be put on such lies.
They are the figments of a sick imagination and should be
dismissed as such, and with the utmost contempt. But whilst
I dismiss the story of the burning house, I cannot as easily
dismiss what happened next. The eleven men in the house
emerged shortly afterwards, made their way into the Temple
court, pushed through the crowd, mounted the steps and turned
to address the people. Some of my priests who were present
on duty (I myself was at prayer at the time) have told me

that the ring-leader, a fisherman from Galilee called
Simon Johnson (his official name. Apparently he is nicknamed
Peter for reasons that escape me) harangued the crowd in a
most seditious and blasphemous manner, claiming that Jesus
Davidson is none other than God himself, come back now as
he promised to set the people free. He even had the
effrontery to quote our holy Scripture to substantiate his
absurd statement. Surely the ultimate blasphemy.

I cannot apologise too deeply for all this. We should,
as I now realise, have been prepared for something of the
sort. The hold Jesus had on the common people was very
strong indeed and we ought to have expected a reaction
following his crucifixion. But I must confess to being taken
completely by surprise by the behaviour of these men.
Johnson himself, on the night of Jesus' arrest, was at pains
to deny publicly and vehemently all knowledge of him. Not
really surprising. He is one of those people who are full
of bluster and self-assurance until a crisis, when they
prove to be men of straw. What is surprising is the boldness
of his behaviour yesterday. We have, of course, been
searching for him these last seven weeks, without success.
He has kept a very low profile indeed and none of our enquiries
elicited any clue as to his whereabouts. So it is all the
more astonishing now to find him so blatantly - and indeed,
to be absolutely fair to the wretched man, fearlessly - out
in the open.

It is unfortunate that we were not able to apprehend him
yesterday. It was a **golden** opportunity to grab the whole
sorry bunch and clap them into prison where they properly

belong. I regret we did not seize it. Within minutes, after he had finished speaking, they were all lost in the crowd. So far it has not been possible to locate them. But it is only a matter of time. Within the next couple of days the city will be empty as the people return to their villages. Then we shall quickly find our quarry. I have no doubt of that.

This man I have put in charge of the operation is extremely efficient and refreshingly enthusiastic about his task. His name is Saul - a young man from Tarsus. A product of one of our finest Torah schools, well-versed in our Law, dedicated and single-minded. He is zealous for the good name of our Faith almost to the point of obsession. He brings to his task a brilliance of mind coupled with a kind of ruthlessness which cannot help but get results. And get them quickly. I am confident that before the week is out we shall have these eleven trouble-makers under lock and key. I have promised the Sanhedrin that they will be given a full trial - the outcome of which I think Your Excellency can predict with absolute certainty.

I trust this will ease your very natural anxieties. I admit the latent seriousness of the situation but I do assure Your Excellency there is no cause for alarm. None whatsoever. Six months from now - less, even - the name of Jesus Davidson will have dropped out of history. For good.

I am, sir,
Your obedient servant,

Caiaphas

Caiaphas.
High Priest.

COMPILER'S NOTE

Readers may be interested to check the biblical
references out of which the material in this file
very largely stems.   They are:

3   Matthew 2.   1-12

4   Luke 2.   8-20

5   Matthew 2.   16-18

6   Luke 2.   8-14

7   Matthew 2.   19-21

8   Luke 2.   41-50

9   Luke 4.   1-13

10   John 2.   1-11

11   John 3.   1-12

12   Matthew 8.   5-13

13   Luke 7.   11-15

14   Luke 4.   31-37

15   Mark 5.   1-17

16   Luke 9.   37-43

17   Matthew 19.   16-22

18   Luke 18.   35-42

19   John 18.   28-19.16

20   Matthew 27.   3-5

21   Mark 15.   6-15

22   John 19.   23-24

23   John 20.   11-18

24   Matthew 28.   11-15

25   Luke 22.   50-51

26   Matthew 27.   57-60

27   Luke 23.   44-47

28   Acts 4.   1-3

29   Acts 2.   1-12

Stuart Jackman